Alliance

La Famiglia

CARMINE COSTELLO

CATERINA & AL RICCI

CARLOTTA & DAMIEN ROMANO

MARCUS RICCI

LILY ROMANO

MADALENA RICCI

LANA ROMANO

Costello

ELIZABETTA COSTELLO

COSETTA & JAMES
VITALE

CARMINE JR. & GIULIA
COSTELLO

JOHNATHAN VITALE

SAM COSTELLO

Playlist

GRAVEYARD. HALSEY
ST. JUDE. FLORENCE AND THE MACHINE
FOREVER FIFTEEN. MOTHICA
PLAY WITH FIRE. SAM TINNESZ
IVY. TAYLOR SWIFT
FRANK OCEAN. CALL ME KARIZMA
I'M OK. CALL ME KARIZMA
MIND IS A PRISON. ALEC BENJAMIN
NO ONE'S IN THE ROOM. JESSIE REYEZ
WORTH SAVING. JESSIE REYEZ
DOLLHOUSE. MELANIE MARTINEZ
I FEEL LIKE I'M DROWNING. TWO FEET
SEX. EDEN
LOVER. TAYLOR SWIFT

Alliance

Editing: Heart Full of Reads
Cover Design: Natalia Lourose
Formatting: Natalia Lourose

TO MY DEPRESION,
SCREW YOU.

DYING IS THE EASY PART,
LIVING IS THE TRICK.

-ATTICUS

PROLOGUE

Lana

BEFORE THE INCIDENT, I HAD never given much thought to what sound a skull would make as it'd hit the pavement, falling from a third floor balcony.

But now, that was the noise that lived in my mind, playing on repeat at any chance it got. Instead of ghosts, I was haunted by an echo.

You could say I've clung on to the odd memories of that night.

The scent of her rose and bergamot perfume lingering in the air, the honey-colored wisps of her hair flowing behind her. I think about her outfit, a pretty summer dress that moved with the breeze. My sister looked hauntingly beautiful for her meeting with death.

In my memories, I can see her swinging her legs over the iron railing. I don't think she notices me entering her room; her eyes looking forward as she lets go, free falling. From that second, my recollections of that night blur. The edges cracked, the images distorted, I don't know what happens next.

I remember my parents. My mother lets loose a shrill scream as she rushes toward the balcony. I often wonder what she thought she could do. Reach out and grab Lily? It was too late. She was already gone.

My mind raced to think about how high of a fall it would be from her balcony to the concrete slab below her. Three floors, maybe nine feet for each level, or is it more? The first floor has taller ceilings... so maybe it's over thirty feet. Can you hear a body smack against the pavement from that height?

Regardless, I did. I heard the sound of her skull cracking. Whether it's a figment of my imagination or not, I can't tell.

My back hit the pale-pink painted walls of my sister's room as I slid down to the ground, wrapping my arms around my knees, rocking back and forth in shock. I wish I could say I did something more heroic as my sister took her last breaths, but I didn't. Instead, I curled into a ball and let the numbness take over.

I often revisit this moment, wondering if there

was something I could have done. Some way I could have prevented this.

But how can you prevent a suicide that you had no idea was coming?

My sister, my best friend, was gone and I had no idea why she did it.

Chills skated over my arms, goosebumps rising on my skin. My chest stopped moving, my lungs refusing to suck in oxygen. My whole world was crashing down, starting from the second she swung her legs over that iron railing.

This is the moment everything changes, everything shifts, a new reality is created, and I am irrevocably broken.

I remember the sounds.

Crying...no, wailing. It's my mother, her thin arms flung over the metal banister, it's the only thing supporting her weight as she cries out into the sky.

My father says something, but I can't pull it out of my memory; can't hear the words.

Strong arms reach forward, and I realize he's shaking me. There's a ringing in my ears. Sometimes I can still hear it if I relive too many of the memories at the same time.

The memories I have are reserved for private moments when I'm tucked behind a locked door and it's safe to let the tears flow. I can't recall them all at once. My heart rate will spike, the tears will blur my eyes. Instead, I have to separate them, mourning small moments — one at a time.

It's an audible click before all the sounds of the room come rushing back. I was in a haze.

I don't remember when *he* enters her room. Dressed in all black with shiny leather loafers crossing the floor. He looks over the balcony, presumably down at Lily's mangled body. I watch his face; he doesn't even grimace when he sees her there. A sick part of me wants to know what he saw. What did my sister's body look like sprawled out on the pavement? Were her bones protruding from the skin, limbs twisted in unnatural ways?

"Well, then…" *he* purrs, his voice just slightly annoyed by the situation at hand. "Guess that won't work."

"Is she okay?" It's a new voice that assaults my senses now.

This is the memory I hate the most. Because while my sister had just died, my eyes lock onto the stranger. Taking in his tanned skin, the flecks of black ink peeking beneath his button-down shirt, the light stubble covering his jaw. He's wearing a gold saint pendant, not all that odd for Italian men but his looks worn and dirty, as if his fingers had been rubbing over the charm for years.

"I don't know," my father hisses, the cool air of his breath hits my cheek, and like a reminder I suck in my own breath of air.

"Jesus, Lana!" His eyes close for a second, as if he's relieved to see me respond, to *breathe*.

The other man has his hand on my shoulder and his warm brown eyes are peering into mine. I want to lose myself in the swirls of chocolate and gold if only to avoid that situation unfolding around me. "Are you okay?" he asks, a slight drawl to his words.

"I don't know."

I'll repeat this answer for the next few years to everyone who asks.

I think I'm okay. My body is here. My heart is beating, my lungs are sucking in air. Physically, I'm fine.

Mentally, well, mentally, I saw my sister take her final leap.

I don't think I'll ever be "okay" again.

CHAPTER ONE

Lana

THE DAY MY GRANDFATHER DIES, I know my protection will be buried with him.

I want to sit and cry, to wallow in the pain of losing my favorite person, my biggest supporter, but my parents have a gleam in their eyes, and the whispering has started. I'm certain they have a plan, and I'm just as sure I won't like it. Knowing my parents, they won't stop until they get what they want.

And what they want is an alliance.

Even at my grandfather's funeral, my mother is plotting. A symptom of growing up in the Costello *Famiglia*, I assume. For the past three years, Carlotta Costello has been a tigress, lying in wait, searching for a weakness in her prey she can exploit. She walks into her father's funeral with the confidence of a man in a suit. Despite being raised by her, I've never spent a day with the prowess my mother has.

Suddenly my black dress feels suffocating. It's a warm day for December in New Orleans, the temperature reaching the low seventies. The French Quarter is lit up, holiday decor dons every building, lights are strewn across the streets. But inside the walls of this funeral home, all festiveness ceases to exist.

Funerals and I don't do well together. Memories of Lily's float through my head, making me dizzy. The thoughts don't bode well with me as I recall the screaming matches between my mom and her siblings. My mother wasn't one to accept any faults of her own. She refused to acknowledge that her actions had anything to do with her daughter's death. Instead of accepting any blame, she let the crater between her and her siblings expand, creating a large division right down the middle of our family.

The only one to end the commotion was my grandfather. I spare a glance at his coffin; I guess he won't be here to help now.

The Costello siblings have a rocky history of getting along, even before Lily's death. Love didn't flow freely between the four of them. Mostly, they conspire with whoever has their back at the moment. I glance at my parents huddled with Aunt Caterina. This tells me she's their current ally.

Of the four Costello children, my mother has always been the closest with her older sister. The younger two siblings, Aunt Cosetta and Uncle Carmine, tend to leave out their older sisters. It feels like a civil war divided the two pairs, forcing the four siblings to constantly be at odds with each other.

The only time they tolerated each other's presence was around my grandfather, Carmine Costello Sr.

Grandpapa had a low threshold for the fights between siblings, whether it was my mom and her siblings, or me and Lily. His view was that family should stick together. If only he knew his children were just sitting around waiting for him to die, so they could burn his beloved city to the ground with their petty war.

They can't even wait for the funeral to be over.

Each of them is dying to take over New Orleans. The only thing the four siblings have in common is that none of them are willing to let anything impede their plans. Even each other.

As if on cue, Uncle Carmine aka Junior, the chosen successor, walks through the wooden door leading into the funeral home. Dressed impeccably in a black three-piece suit and his salt and pepper hair slicked back, he looks like a younger version of my grandfather. Behind him is his son, Sam, the spitting image of his father.

Despite the plotting currently happening in the room's corner, Uncle Junior has been running *La famiglia* for a while now. Since before Grandpapa's diagnosis, before the chemo, and before the month of hospice.

Uncle Junior's eyes immediately find my mother and Aunt Caterina in the corner and both straighten their spines as he approaches them. I stand on the balls of my feet, clutching the paper cup of water I'm holding, ready for the shouting to start.

I think everyone in the room is bracing themselves.

It's well known in the family that Uncle Junior doesn't care for his two older sisters, and now that Grandpapa is gone, he has no reason to support them.

I swallow hard as he approaches, looking at my mother and Aunt Caterina up and down. I can't hear what he whispers, but the scowl on Aunt Caterina's face tells me she's not thrilled.

My mother straightens her spine, her tell that she's feeling defensive, and my father has his lips pursed into a thin line.

Despite my mother's lifelong goal of pleasing her

father, she married a man that he didn't like. Maybe it wasn't that he didn't like him as much as he saw through his motives. Hell, half of New Orleans can see through Damien Romano's motives. He's transparent, and it's clear his intention is to take the boss's seat.

"You look nervous."

I turn my head quickly to lock eyes with Sam. I was so focused on my parents' body language that I didn't notice him creep up on me.

"I'm not," I spit out with more venom than I mean to.

Sam smirks and shoves his hands into the pockets of his Tom Ford dress slacks. He leans his back against the wall that I'm standing by. "You know what they want to do?" he asks.

Despite our parents' hatred of each other, Sam has been nothing but kind to me our entire lives. He's seven years older than me, three years older than Lily is. *Or was.* The two of them were protective of me since the day I was born, always keeping me under their wings and looking out for me.

I look over at him, his features are serious, questioning.

"I have an idea," I tell him. "Same thing they tried to do to Lily."

He nods his head, confirming my suspicions while his eyes stay glued on our parents. "You want that?" he asks.

I think of Lily. She tried to put on a brave face. I recall her wearing a royal blue dress and nude heels. Her hair was curled perfectly. *"It's gonna be fine, Little Lana."* She had told me with a smile. But whatever *he* did to her that day was not fine.

It pushed her over the edge.

I swallow the lump building in my throat and turn my gaze to meet Sam's. "No," I whisper.

One hand leaves his pocket, coming up to run through the strands of his dark hair. "I didn't think so," he tells me. "You trust me?"

I nod.

"Good." With that, he pushes off the wall and leaves me.

My heart is thrumming in my chest, beating far too fast as I watch the argument transpiring between my uncle and my parents. I do know what they want from me, why I'm sure they're arguing with Uncle Junior. I'm not as dense as most people think. They see a pretty girl with dark hair and wide eyes, and immediately assume I'm some kind of damsel in distress. And that's what I was raised to be, a woman with no goals, just a pretty face.

I feel like I'm suffocating beneath the fabric of my dress. Suddenly the funeral is too overwhelming, too stuffy. I break through the glass French doors, pushing out onto the back patio, heaving in a breath. I suck in air like I haven't breathed in years.

I pant hard as I lean against the brick exterior, letting the rough surface scrape against my bare arm. I need more air. I need everything to stop spinning. It feels as if it's all going to come crashing down at any second.

I'm terrified.

Lily was far stronger than me, she was also the smarter one, the more put-together one. If she couldn't handle this…how will I?

"Are you okay?"

I shake my head without raising it to see who asked the question. It's my least favorite one. Of all the questions to ask, why that?

The truth is, I'm not okay and I haven't been for a while. Maybe since before Lily's death. I'm not even sure 'okay' is a possibility in this family. Most days I strive for fine.

But how am I supposed to be? Should I fake happy, a smile plastered over my face to appease everyone around me? I've attended too many funerals. More than I can count on a single hand, maybe even both hands. How can I be content with the life I've been given when I hate everything about it? How does anyone expect me to be *content* while death piles up around me?

I hiccup a sob, my thoughts pulling the emotions from me and shedding them via water droplets rolling down my cheeks.

"Are you okay?"

The voice asks again, and this time I lift my gaze to see who it is.

Gold pendant. Black ink. Stubbled jawline. Brown eyes.

I look him over twice.

I know him, he was there the night my sister leaped to her death.

CHAPTER TWO

Naz

DECIDEDLY, I AM NOT A good man. Because when I look at the Romano girl standing before me with her hands on her knees, panting her way through a panic attack, the first thing I think is *she's even prettier than she was three years ago.* Which seems like a shitty thing to think about a girl who is on the verge of crying.

"Are you okay?" I ask, and finally those hazel eyes rise to look at me. I see the flecks of gold dancing in her vision, fucking beautiful, just like that last time I saw her.

Apparently, I have a penchant for finding her at the worst moments. I think back to the last time I talked to her. She was in the midst of a spiral, her arms wrapped around her knees, her breathing uneven. I asked her the same question then too.

I felt stupid immediately after the words left my lips. She probably wasn't okay, considering the tragedy she had just seen, but still I asked the question.

"Fine," she breathes out. "I'm fine."

She's not fine. Her eyes are glassy, there's a hand clenched to her stomach. I can tell by the look in her eyes that she's still in panic mode.

"Here" — I gesture to the wrought-iron table and chairs on the patio behind the funeral home — "sit down."

Begrudgingly, she listens to me, smoothing the skirt of her black dress and sitting on the patio set. I join her silently, considering my words, unsure what the best thing to say to someone who's grieving is.

"I'm sorry," I tell her. "For your loss." I cringe at myself.

Her eyes lift back up to study me, running over my features and settling on the charm dangling from my neck. I bring my hand to it instinctually, rubbing my calloused fingers over the round edges. I've worn the thing for half of my life at this point, using it as an anchor.

"St. Jude," I tell her. "The patron saint of lost causes."

"I'm sorry," she whispers. "I didn't mean to stare."

She averts her gaze from the charm quickly, instead staring at her hands, twisting her fingers together.

"It's fine," I say. "I've had it a long time."

She nods, staying silent for a moment before she finally meets my eyes again. "Why Saint Jude? Why lost causes?"

I chuckle, still running my fingers over the smooth edges of the charm. "My grandmother gave it to me." I shrug. "It sounds bad, I know, but it wasn't. She prayed that Saint Jude would bring me luck, help me out, ya know?"

"Are you a lost cause?" she asks, the gold flecks of her eyes shining brightly.

"Aren't we all?"

She smiles at that, the corners of her lips rising as she releases a small chuckle.

"I'm Lana," she says, extending a manicured hand for me to shake.

"Naz." I meet her hand with mine, shaking it gently.

She looks better now, different from when I first found her. Her poise has returned, her spine has straightened.

"You keep finding me at my worst moments," she says with a soft smile.

"I'm sorry about that," I mutter the words, but

29

I've already thought the same thing. Death follows this girl, and I'm always close behind.

"Don't be. Do you work for my father?"

I cringe at the reminder that I'm just a soldier to her, beneath the ranks of her family. "Your cousin," I answer, "Marcus."

"Ah," she says at the realization. "Is that why you were there that night?"

Even though it was years ago, she doesn't need to explain what night she's referring to, we're both well aware.

"Yes, I came with him." My chest is tightening at this line of questioning. For one reason, I'm not supposed to talk business with women. For another, I'm not made. I'm barely allowed to know about the business, as I'm still proving myself to these men, and fraternizing with the princess isn't going to bode well for me.

But what was I supposed to do? Leave her here crying and just walk past her? I couldn't have done that.

But she's not crying anymore. I know I should get up and excuse myself, but I can't. I'm glued to this chair, feet anchored to the ground. I'm addicted to this conversation, to hearing her voice, watching her face. I can't fucking move.

The Costello family isn't my favorite. Before Marcus hired me, I was quick to avoid them. Growing up poor, surrounded by other poor Italian-Americans, we all heard the stories about their violence. Carmine settled in New Orleans decades ago with his wife before they had their four kids. He built his organization from the ground up, there wasn't a soul in NOLA who didn't know his name.

Including me.

Lana's heart-shaped face and pouty lips don't inherently look dangerous. If I didn't know better, I would think she was just a girl, albeit a beautiful one, but still just a girl. But she's far more than that. She's practically royalty with the Costello blood running through her.

"So you know then?" she asks, her pink lips purse at the question and her hazel eyes watch me, waiting for a response.

My stomach clenches at her question. I know exactly what she's talking about, but I wish I didn't. If I would have never told Marcus I wanted to be made... maybe, then I wouldn't be privy to that information. Maybe I would still be *just* a drug dealer. One who didn't have nightmares of girls falling from balconies.

"Yes," I whisper. I know what she means. I know that her family sucks for what they're doing to her.

I know, and yet I stand by. Because even though I think it's terrible, and even though I wouldn't wish it on my worst enemy — there's nothing I can do.

She nods her head sadly, using her fingertips to push a stray piece of hair from her face. "Is he bad?" Her eyes are pleading with me, begging me to give her something. Some amount of hope.

But I can't give her what she wants.

"Lana," I whisper, "I can't—"

"I know." She waves a hand. "I'm sorry." She looks defeated as her eyes lower to her lap. "I had to try though." She shrugs, and I can't blame her for that. If it were me, I'd probably be running.

"Hey." Before I know what I'm doing, I reach across the space between us and set a hand on her knee in a reassuring gesture. There's a million lines running through my head, thought after thought of things I could say to her. But none of them would bring her comfort, none of them would change her situation or bring her loved ones back from the dead. "I'm sorry." I settle with sympathy.

She gives me a brief smile, a small glimpse at what another version of her would look like. A version that's not crippled with grief and obligations.

I have to shake her from my mind, forget the image of that sad smile.

ALLIANCE

I can't help her. Nobody can.

CHAPTER THREE

Lana

THERE'S A POUNDING IN MY head that matches the pounding on the front door.

I drank too much last night. After the funeral, I snuck a bottle of expensive whiskey from my father's office and drank myself into oblivion in the privacy of my bedroom. A rare act of defiance from me.

Rule breaking was Lily's department. I was the good daughter. The one who listened, wore pretty dresses, and only spoke when spoken to. Lily was wild, wore bright colors and weird prints. She had a habit of asking questions at the most inopportune times, leaving my parents angry with her more often than not.

My heart aches thinking about Lily. Missing her

fills me to the brim, leaving my mind with no room for anything other than sadness. There's too much pain in my head and my heart, and no matter how I try to fill my days, it lingers there, making me feel it all.

There's a saying thrown at me anytime I voice my sadness, that time will heal it. But it's been three years, and I still wake up thinking she'll be in the room next to mine. I don't believe any amount of time will heal me. Heal this.

My parents' grief seemed to end quicker than mine. A week after Lily's death, my mother was pulling all reminders of her from the house and packing them up in unmarked containers to be cast away to the basement. Pictures, momentos, anything that reeked of Lily was gone. We went from a four-person family to three in the blink of an eye.

Just as quickly, all mentions of her vanished with the photos. Her name became a sinful word in the house. No one mentioned her. As if eliminating her name from our vocabulary would somehow make her loss easier on us, more palatable.

I wish I would have spoken up, aired my grievances, but Lily had always been the one to stand up for us. Instead, I packed myself away in my room, not coming out for days on end. Decidedly, if Lily was dead, then I would hole myself up until I was too.

The person to bring me out of my self-induced coma was the next to die, my grandfather.

Only this time, I can't fade away. For one, I knew this was coming, we all did. Five months ago, he called us all over to his estate to tell us he was dying. He hid his cancer from the family for six months before that, privately consulting doctors and weighing his odds before he finally sat us down and broke the news.

He didn't want chemo. Didn't want to die weak and sick. It was my cousin, Madi, who finally talked him into it, but one round, no results, and he was done.

And still, when the call came, it felt like a knife through my heart.

My mother finally answers the door. I hear her muffled greeting slither up the stairs, the sound piercing to my ears. "Lana!" she calls and without thinking, I audibly groan.

The ibuprofen has yet to kick in, and the constant pounding of my head refuses to dull. I showered and dressed an hour ago, but then I curled back up on my bed and stewed in my hangover.

"Lana!" she shouts again when I don't immediately leap from my bed and head to the stairs. With another groan, I swing my legs off the mattress and move toward her calls. The cotton fabric of the charcoal-colored t-shirt dress clings to my back as I make my way downstairs. Despite my mother telling me to look nice, I piled my hair into a bun atop my head and only put on mascara, leaving the remainder of my face bare. This isn't what she meant, nor will it reach her standards, but I'd argue that I've looked worse.

When I meet her downstairs, my father is standing next to her and behind them is a tall, lean man, wearing a tan coat with silver eyes focused on me.

I pause on the steps, taking in his smooth skin leading to his ash brown hair and lightly stubbled jaw. He brings a hand to meet his mouth, running over his full lips and jawline. What's left in its wake is a sinister smirk.

"Darling," my father says, his hand extending to hold mine as I descend the last few steps. "This is Congressman LaFontaine," he says, gesturing with his head toward the previously unknown man in our foyer.

"Please," the congressman interjects, extending his hand to take mine. "Call me Davis."

Those pink lips curl again, rising back into a smirk. I'm sure other women would lose their panties seeing him in their house, knowing their parents are vying to marry them off. Considering the looks and *ages* of other eligible bachelors in Louisiana that would give my parents the clout they're looking for, Congressman LaFontaine is a good option.

But the sight of him there, looking at me as if I'm a meal to be devoured, makes my stomach uneasy.

Davis LaFontaine. The man who was supposed to marry my older sister. After one date with him, she swung her legs over the iron bars of her balcony and fell to her death.

I think about it more often than I'd like to admit. He looks the same as he did that night, when he walked through her bedroom, looked over the side of the balcony and scoffed. I saw the look on his face; he wasn't saddened by her death at all, looking like the whole ordeal was nothing more than an inconvenience to him.

"Davis," I repeat, letting him wrap his smooth hand around mine. Instead of shaking it, he pulls me to him, wrapping the other arm around my waist and hugging me. His hold feels suffocating, and my hand begins to get clammy within his grip.

"Pleased to meet you," he tells me as he releases his hold on me.

The transaction feels slimy, knowing what he's

here for. I wonder what it's like for him, a man ten years my senior, conspiring with my parents to marry me. I wonder if he thinks I'm willing. What would he say if he heard me voice my true feelings?

Something tells me he doesn't care what I think.

"Let's head to the dining room," my mother says in a chipper tone, sending another wave of nausea to my gut. My mother is generally not a chipper person; sly and cunning are more suited descriptions for Carlotta Romano. Anything else is an act, and that means she has an angle. "I made brunch."

My stomach growls in response to the mention of food, and Davis snorts a soft laugh next to me. I haven't eaten since before Grandpapa's funeral yesterday, long before all the liquor I swallowed. My stomach is protesting, begging for something with more substance.

"Sorry," I mutter as we head for the table. Davis brings a hand to the small of my back to lead me there, like this isn't the home I've lived in for twenty years.

Once we're seated, his gaze turns to my father, a smile growing on his handsome face. He looks pleased, which only means that this transaction is moving to the next phase.

That heaviness returns to my gut, making my starving stomach too sick to eat. Davis piles my mother's southern brunch onto his plate. Fried chicken, biscuits, and gravy — a morning meal fit for southern royalty. I skip the chicken and gravy, opting for half a biscuit and a small scoop of eggs. He looks pleased when he eyes the food on my plate.

The problem with men in my family, in this town even, is that they see women as objects to own.

Little dolls that dress nicely and look good on your arm. They require upkeep, healthy diets, and plenty of exercise. Like a dog that needs caring for. But if you give them enough shiny objects and green money, they'll shut up and be quiet.

I've never cared much for shiny things.

"So, Davis, tell us about your work." There's a large, forced grin spread across my mother's cheeks. She doesn't care much for small talk, and seeing as I'm not contributing to the conversation, she's forcing practiced topics to try to make Davis and I bond.

The more excitable I am, the easier this whole ordeal will be.

Using my fork, I push the eggs around on my plate and pretend to listen to Davis talk. He sounds like every other southern politician. A slight Louisiana drawl to his voice, using large words and pretty phrases to distract from what's underneath.

Dark eyes find me as he slices through the meat

41

on his plate. "So, Lana," he drawls, "your father said you're enrolled at Tulane, what are you studying there?"

I'm taken aback when he directs his question to me. "Yeah," I mumble, "uh, English."

He hums a low sound while tapping his finger against his glass. "Interesting," he says, "won't have much use for it, huh?"

His statement hits me like a ton of bricks. I can't come up with a response with his eyes set on me before he moves on, turning back to my father as if he's suddenly bored with me. I have to catch my breath and straighten myself out.

I spare a glance at his handsome face; he's charming enough, but underneath the surface there's something dangerous, I'm sure of it.

Beyond his silver eyes and well-made exterior, there's something shady about Davis LaFontaine.

Davis pats his stomach after he eats, grinning widely at my mother and complimenting her food. My mother didn't cook a thing on the table, but she takes the compliments anyway.

"Can I have a moment with Lana before we make things official?" Davis asks with a smile. He doesn't direct his words to me, instead he looks to my father for permission.

The whole thing makes me feel like there's an invisible leash wrapped around my neck and my father is handing the reins over to the new owner. Dad smiles at Davis, clapping a hand on his shoulder in a show of solidarity.

With a hand pressed to my lower back, Davis leads me into the formal living room. The space is decorated for Christmas, a large ten-foot tree stands in front of the picture windows, adorned with gold ornaments and red ribbons. Growing up, Lily and I loved Christmas. The house was always decorated perfectly, presents sat under the tree, and the entire family came together. Now, I feel a chill run over my skin at the thought. No Lily. No Grandpapa. No family. I rub the goosebumps away with the palms of my hands. If Davis notices, he doesn't comment on it.

"So, Lana," he says my name with a chilling smirk plastered on his face. "It feels like you're not interested in me, hmm?" It's a weirdly phrased question, paired with his silver eyes throwing daggers at me.

In an attempt to gain some space between us, my feet step back, but Davis is quicker than me. He captures my arm in his hand and pulls my body closer to him, holding me hostage in his grip.

"Tell me," he sneers, his lips curving around the

words. "Are you going to be a pain in my ass like your older sister?" His grip on my arm tightens to a punishing pain as the threatening words leave his lips with droplets of saliva.

"I—" I choke on the words, taken aback by his sudden forcefulness. Gone is the man who just ate a plateful of fried chicken and biscuits at my dining room table. "I don't know what you're talking about!" I nearly shout at him, tugging on my arm in a feeble attempt to free myself from his grip.

"Stupid girl," he mocks. "I require very little from you. Be quiet, behave, and walk down the aisle in a pretty little dress. If you do as I say, I'll reward you, if you fail... well..."

In perfect timing, he squeezes my arm with punishing forcefulness as if making a promise for future pain if I disobey.

Tears begin to well in my eyes as I look up at his menacing face. I'm not sure what I've ever done to make this man so hateful, other than be born with a vagina in place of a dick.

"Don't cry, baby," he taunts, lifting his finger to delicately wipe my tears away, a confusing gesture in comparison to the pain he just inflicted on me. "Just behave. Do I make myself clear?" he asks, those silver eyes digging deep into my soul, waiting for my answer, my commitment to him.

I nod, if only to get him off me, to gain space between us so I can breathe and think again. With my agreement, he drops his grip on my arm, and instinctively I reach for it with my opposite hand, running it over the reddened flesh.

I want to cry and scream, do anything other than stand here and take the abuse. But the southern belle inside of me, the girl they raised me to be, can't move from this spot standing in front of the Christmas tree. My hatred for this man and love for this holiday begin to mix, swirling around and staining everything with bitterness. I don't have words to express myself, no vocabulary to tell him to leave me alone or fuck off. I stand there like a scared child waiting for the burst of abuse and love, the two emotions so entangled together.

Davis flexes his hand, as if causing me pain has hurt him. He reaches into his suit pocket, withdrawing a black velvet box and popping it open. Inside sits a diamond, far too large for my finger. With no words, he plucks the ring from its cozy home and grabs my hand. He slides the gold band with the heavy diamond onto my finger. Afterward, he snaps the box shut and deposits it back into his suit jacket, walking away, leaving me flushed and empty.

Merry Christmas to me.

CHAPTER FOUR

Naz

"YOU WANT SOME?" JASON, ONE of my regulars, extends his rolled up dollar bill to me and gestures to the white lines that lay on top of the coffee table with a flick of his eyes.

In my weaker moments, I've dropped to my knees, stuffed the dirty dollar into my nostrils and snorted deeply. Letting the white powder ease my nerves and erase my mind was not the best coping mechanism of mine. Ditching the powder was no easy feat, but luckily, unlike Jason, I stopped before the addiction got too bad. My motivation came from looking in the mirror and only seeing a younger version of my father.

His paper-thin hand shakes while he extends it to me, the loose skin from all the weight he's lost jiggling with the motion. Once upon a time he was probably a bright kid, now he's an addict.

As long as he places the stack of bills in my hand, it's not my place to judge. I'm just here to hand over the product and leave him to his vices.

"Nah." I shake my head. He bumps it, tipping his head back after snorting the powder and moaning in pleasure. There's always a sickness that rolls through my stomach when I watch others take drugs. I think I should feel worse, guilt or shame, something to stop me from continuing to enable the addicts that find me. But I can't. Because the money they put in my hands is worth more to me than doing the right thing.

"That's good," he tells me, his hand fishing in his pocket for the pile of money he owes me. Pulling the wrinkled bills out, he slaps them into my outstretched palm. I shove the cash in my pocket. Somewhere in the background I can hear a baby cry, and I shudder. Weeks from Christmas and this man is spending money on coke rather than providing for his baby.

Without commenting, I leave the house and head back out into the Lower Ninth Ward. I keep my eyes peeled as I move down the street to my next drop. I've been working for Marcus Ricci for a few years now, and I'm still stuck with the Lower Ninth Ward, Central City, and The Garden District—the parts of town that no one wants. The money is still good, but the clientele is slowly fading away, falling victim to the drugs. The only bright side is they're less likely to end up in rehab.

I don't complain though. I'll work any street Marcus puts me on with a smile on my face. As long as the money keeps finding its way into my pocket, I'll keep showing up.

Marcus picked me up out of a club where I was working the door. He saw me bouncing a few junkies and offered me a job. I wonder sometimes if he could see the desperation on my face, the need for money so strong it was the only thought that flowed through my brain. Maybe he preys on kids like me. Kids with Italian genes and bank accounts in the negatives, the perfect soldiers.

As if on cue, my phone rings, boasting Marcus' name on the caller ID. "Yeah?" I answer.

"Got time for an event tonight?" His voice rings through the speaker.

Flicking my wrist, I check the time on my watch. I need to stop by Ma's, but I know this isn't a real question from him. The answer has to be yes. I don't get a choice while working for my button, my key into the Costello *Famiglia*. I do as the made men ask, whenever they ask, and pray that sooner rather than later, they initiate me into this thing.

This thing of ours, this secret society is the only thing that's kept me above water. And if they initiate me, I won't have to worry about money ever again.

"Yeah," I tell him. "Where at?"

Marcus rattles off the address and I make a mental note of the location. It's in the French Quarter, a private party at some club, looking for hookup. I'll need to make my stop at Ma's quick, change my clothes and head out.

I reach for the keys in my pocket and head for the new Jeep Wrangler parked on South Street. One of the many perks of working for Marcus is that the money is steady, coming in quicker than I can spend it. For the first time in my life, I have a nice car that won't break down every ten miles.

Another perk of the money is being able to lay an envelope of cash on my mother's kitchen table, knowing that I can still buy groceries for myself and pay my rent.

Whoever said money can't buy happiness clearly had money.

"I don't want that," Ma tells me without even turning around to see the envelope. She swipes a hand through her graying hair while the other one stirs the pot of red sauce bubbling on the stove top.

"What do you mean you don't want it?" I ask with

a scoff, not bothering to pick the envelope back up.

This is an ongoing occurrence. She likes to fret about taking the money, claiming it's corrupt and evil, but at the end of the night, I'll leave the envelope there, and she'll spend it because she has no other choice.

Before she can continue her onslaught of reasons why she doesn't want the gift I just presented to her, Anthony bolts from the back room heading toward me at full force. He wraps his arms around my waist, his small head hitting my abdomen.

"Naz, Ma got me a new game, you wanna play?" He's a happy kid, looking up at me with a slight smile and bright eyes. He's better than I was at that age, though I'd argue that not starving and living in a nicer home plays a role in his disposition.

"Sorry, bud," I tell him, patting his back with the palm of my hand. "Where's Elly?" I ask Ma.

Elly, my younger sister, had Anthony before she graduated high school, much to my mother's disappointment. She's not a bad mother, just young and inexperienced. Being poor and having the kid's father run out just didn't help much either.

"Work," Ma grumbles, bringing a spoonful of sauce to her lips. "She works too much."

I sigh, my eyes flickering to the envelope of cash

on the table. "She doesn't need to work. I'm taking care of it." I've told my sister more times than I can count that she doesn't need a job, that she should be home with Anthony. I steady my nerves as I head for my old room at the back, hoping I have something in there I can wear to the club.

No matter how much cash I leave on that table, and how many times they use it, they still act too good for it. I'm a disappointment in my mother's eyes, no matter how much money I provide for them, how much better off they are. Anthony has food on the table, video games to play, a nice home—yet still my line of work is shameful.

I can't blame them. I won't say I'm a saint, but I'm a provider, and that can't be denied.

There's a black button-down shirt in the closet that I pull over my white t-shirt, pairing it with the black jeans that I'm already wearing. Checking my appearance in the mirror, I slick back my hair and run my fingertips over the St. Jude pendant. I look good enough.

I head back out to the kitchen, pressing a quick kiss to the back of my mother's head.

"Use the money, Ma."

Royal is in the heart of the French Quarter, a two-story club blasting music so loudly it flows out onto the street.

There's a bouncer ushering the patrons into the correct areas. Downstairs is the general admission, filled with tourists hoping to get their fill of the Big Easy. Upstairs in the private part, NOLA lifers get their rocks off and take home the tourists to spend the night in their beds.

Private parties, clubs, tourists — they all bring me good money. Each one craving drugs and willing to put bills in my pocket in exchange for their vice of choice.

Plant, powder, or pills.

There's a satchel hanging from my shoulder, filled with the goods. The bouncer waves me through, expecting me probably after receiving a call from Marcus. The Costellos run the Quarter, and Marcus has his hands in every nook and cranny of the business, even the parts where he's unwanted.

The place is bedecked for Christmas, filled with cheerfulness. Christmas trees with shatterproof ornaments sit on each floor. Festive garland is wrapped around the balcony, puffy white cotton, glittered, giving off a snowy look and sitting atop every surface.

I'm waved over by a girl, Lynn, I think that's what her name is. Someone Marcus fucks, I'm pretty sure.

She smiles eagerly at me and rattles off her poison before I'm even over to her. I pull the white tablet she wants from my bag and hand it over in exchange for the cash she slips into my palm.

Lynn is the first of many, each asking for some type of escape that I'm more than willing to supply. I sip a whiskey on the rocks while I watch the scene of young adults lounging on velvet sofas unfold in front of me.

Rich kids are good business. They shell out handfuls of money for drugs that help them escape their imaginary problems. Sometimes I think they take the drugs just so they could have a problem, something to be worried or concerned about. Fabricated issues just to make themselves feel something.

I've felt enough for a lifetime. The only drug I dabble with these days is pot. I need the downers to help me sleep, to ease the anxiety that claws at me all day. I don't smoke while I'm working though; I reserve it for my nights off in the comfort of my bed.

I'm about to head out when I see a familiar dark head of hair enter the club. Copper highlights shine against the lights and slim legs lead her up the stairs. She stops when she reaches the top, pursing her lips. She looks out of place, not dressed up enough for the rest of the people here. She wears a dark colored t-shirt dress, her hair piled in a bun on top of her head, and instead of high heels she wears a pair of black Converse. Beside her, a girl in an ugly Christmas sweater drags her to the bar, pulling up alongside me.

While her friend spouts off an order to the bartender, Lana's eyes finally find me. They start at my shoes, the pair of black ankle boots, and scan up my jeans and shirt before settling on my face. "Naz," she says softly, a smile rising on her lips.

"Lana."

Her smile only grows when I say her name. "What are you doing here?" she asks, cocking her head to the side.

The question makes me uneasy, unsure what to tell her. The truth is work, but she knows exactly what that means and for some reason pointing out to this girl that I'm a drug dealer just doesn't seem smart.

The friend in the ugly sweater turns suddenly, handing a glass filled with ice and liquor to Lana. "Molly." She extends her hand for me, almost instinctively I reach into my bag to find her a dose before quickly realizing she's telling me her name.

I wait for her to walk away, called over by another girl who screeches her name loudly. Lana's eyes are still trained on me. "So," she says, barely loud enough for me to hear her over the music. Her eyes move to the bag on my shoulder then back to my face. "Working?" she asks, and I'm glad she brings it up first.

"Yep."

She takes a sip of her drink, wrapping her full lips around the plastic straw. There's a beast inside of me that comes to life at the action, watching her suck the liquid from the cup, imagining those lips wrapped around my cock. I try to shake the dirty image from my mind.

Her fingers poke at a clump of the white glittery cotton. "Have you ever seen *real* snow?" she asks with the curiosity of a small child.

"No," I tell her. "But I hear it's annoying as fuck."

Hazel eyes shoot up to mine and a laugh bursts from her lips. "I'd like to see it," she tells me. "It sounds magical." She says the word with a sense of idealism I envy. As if she can see all the beauty in the world, while I'm left here seeing everything as only white or black, good or bad.

She takes another gulp of her liquid courage, grimacing as it slides down her throat.

"Bad day?" I ask, my eyes flashing to her half-empty glass.

Those hazel eyes fly up to meet mine, the flecks of gold shining in the flashing lights. "Terrible," she says, and for some reason I love the way that word sounds on her lips. I want to ease her of her demons, make her day better.

"Can I remedy it?" I ask her, leaning in closer, enough to smell the honey and lavender scent of her hair.

Her breath comes out in a heavy pant and for a minute I think she'll tell me to fuck off, but she doesn't. "Yeah, can we get out of here?"

CHAPTER FIVE

Lana

NAZ DOESN'T WASTE A MOMENT once the words leave my lips. He ushers me outside the club, to a shiny black Jeep parked on the street. With a click of the key fob, the lights come to life and the car unlocks. He lifts me into the passenger seat with such ease before rounding the car and hopping into the driver's side.

"Where to?" he asks, the engine roaring to life.

"Far," I say, and I'm met with a chuckle.

"What are you trying to escape, *bella?*" He doesn't put the car in drive, instead he removes his hand from the gearshift and turns his attention on me. His warm eyes penetrate me, seeing through my brittle exterior, past the façade that my family has created.

What am I trying to escape?

I play with the idea of telling him about my arranged marriage. About the ring that I have stuffed in my underwear drawer back home. About my parents who showed no sympathy when I came back to the kitchen with an angry red mark blooming on my arm.

Today, for the first time since her death, I felt angry with Lily. She met this man and took the easy way out; she jumped to escape him and with her escape she put me directly in the path of the lion.

I want to tell Naz all of this. All the thoughts spiraling through my head that led me to calling Molly and leaving my house tonight.

I don't though, out of fear that he'll call me naïve.

A stupid, silly girl.

I was raised in this town, in this family. I know how the game works, I know the power plays, and yet I thought that behaving and looking pretty would somehow exempt me from them.

And what would he say to me? There's nothing he can do to change this, to fix this broken situation. He knows. I know he knows what my family plans to do. If he's a true soldier, he'll probably drive me right back home, dropping me off on the front porch with a bow.

Those deep eyes are studying me as the thoughts roll through my head, threatening to take over and send me back into a panic. His tattooed hand reaches up to his throat, his thumb and forefinger slipping over the St. Jude pendant. I don't think he even notices that he does it, it's just an instinct.

Naz is handsome in a bad boy way. He's not the type of man my parents would ever approve of. The black ink that peeks out of his button-down shirt, working its way toward his throat, would give my mother a heart attack. Even his fingers are covered, the ink extending toward his nail beds. For some reason that I can't place, it sends a rush of heat to my core.

His hair is slicked back, dark as black ink, and buzzed on either side. He looks well-groomed but there's a few days' worth of stubble that covers his chin and my mind wanders to thoughts of how it would feel between my thighs.

"Everything," I finally answer his question. "I'm trying to escape everything."

He moves a hand to his face, rubbing over his chin thoughtfully. I don't want him to overthink this. I want him to take me home; I want to feel him between my legs, his mouth on my skin; I want to erase Davis' hand from my body; I want to experience a man that I choose.

And I definitely did not choose Davis LaFontaine.

"Take me to your house," I breathe. "Please."

Wordlessly, he does. Bringing me to a newly built apartment building, an old five-story parking garage turned into rentals. The building has an edge to it and once we get to his unit I'm met with a large open-living space with an industrial feel. The ceilings are tall and the windows are huge, letting the silver light of the moon cast its glow on the hardwoods.

I'm barely inside the space before he has me pressed against the wall, one hand roaming the side of my body while the other comes to palm my cheek. The warmth of his skin permeates my soul, igniting parts of myself I hadn't realized were cold and dying until his fire was licking at my flesh.

Warm, full lips come to mine, pressing against me softly at first, and then harder. Taking everything I have to give. I meet him there, tongue for tongue, war for war. I give myself over to him, willingly, longing to feel everything I've been missing.

Longing for that spark, that fire, knowing that this might be the only time in my life I experience it.

The hand on my side snakes lower and then tugs at the hem of my dress before going underneath the fabric. I suck in a harsh breath as he comes closer to my core, every nerve in my body on edge, waiting for that friction it desperately wants.

Fingers graze my center over my panties, making me whine with anticipation.

Tattoos stretch across his body, black ink that whirls and moves fluidly over his tanned skin. I want to trace every inch of the ink, decode every design that marks his body. I writhe beneath him, against the wall, a small whine leaving my lips as I buck my hips, searching for any amount of friction I can get.

"Patience," his raspy voice tells me, a smirk rising on his lips.

I have none of that, I want him there now. I want all of him, everything he has to give. I need to feel.

Him.

Everything.

I need it all.

The uncertainty of my future is hovering over me, making everything feel like a last opportunity. Like this might be the last time I get to be with someone I choose, with someone who doesn't see me as a bargaining chip.

"Please," I beg, bringing my own hand on top of his, trying furtively to bring his fingers where I desperately want them.

"Lana," he admonishes me, but my name on his lips sounds perfect. "Are you sure, *angel?*"

Angel.

I don't feel like an angel. I don't feel like the type of good girl who deserves that pet name. I'm out here betraying my family, doing something I know I shouldn't be.

But right now, I'm choosing this. Deciding to be in this moment, here with him.

"Yeah," I breathe out. "I'm sure."

He doesn't ask again, instead letting his fingers drift under the band of my thong. A boot-clad foot comes between my black Converse and with a tap he instructs me to widen my stance. I oblige.

Power doesn't always come from being the loudest, the strongest, the one with most control. Sometimes, it comes from letting go.

And with Naz, I let go.

I let him take control of the moment. He uses my widened stance to get better access to my pussy, spreading my lips and dragging his finger through my wetness.

"Pretty girl," he purrs, bringing the digit to my swollen clit. "You're all turned on for me?"

I can feel the heat rise to my cheeks from his words, feeling dirty beneath his grasp, but only for a minute. He draws lazy circles around the bundle of nerves with his finger while his other hand rakes through my hair. He brings his lips to my ear, the stubble scratching across my cheek. "Can you be a good girl for me?" he asks, his voice barely above a whisper.

I nod enthusiastically, ready for him to take me. His fingers pinch my clit, making me gasp loudly, before he pulls them away. "Words, *angel*. I want to hear you."

"Yes," I say frantically, begging for the stimulation to return. "Yes, I can be a good girl."

He tugs at the hem of my dress, lifting it over my head and casting it aside. Brown eyes peer down at me, beaming with pride. "On your knees," he demands, and I drop, letting my knees hit the hardwood floor of his apartment, eagerly awaiting what comes next.

Naz unbuttons his shirt, tossing it to the floor before he unzips his black jeans, letting them fall and kicking them off along with his shoes. His boxers follow quickly, until he stands bare before me.

He strokes his considerable length with one hand while the other grasps my hair. I waste no time, and leaning forward, I lick down his shaft. When I hear moans escaping from above me, I continue, licking the length of his cock before taking the tip into my mouth.

I suck and tease for as long as possible, until his

hand tugs on my hair and pulls me off him. I'm grinning, claiming victory with his panting. I can tell he's stopping himself from coming down my throat as he leads me to the bed, pushing me so I'm on all fours on the mattress.

He leaves me there for a moment, yanking open the drawer of his night stand and digging out a foil packet. When he returns, he slides the rubber up the length of his cock before bringing himself to my entrance. He drags the head of his cock through my wetness, coating himself. "You ready, baby?" he asks, and I peek over my shoulder to see the cocky grin rising on his cheeks.

With slow movements, he eases inside me, stretching me to accommodate his width. Once he's in, he's ruthless in his pounding. His name leaves my lips with a curse followed by a moan. Tattooed fingers reach around, finding my sensitive nub and drawing quick circles, making me scream out.

"That's right, baby," he groans above me. "Scream my name. Yell it as loud as possible so everyone knows who's fucking you right now."

His words send me over the edge, his name leaving my lips like a prayer with every thrust. When he's close, he pulls out of me ripping the condom off and spilling his cum onto my back.

ALLIANCE

We lay there like that, panting and sticky with cum and sweat. Our hearts light and our minds free from all expectations and obligations.

Hours later, we do it again and again, until we're drunk on orgasms, exhausted and fully sated.

Within the four walls of his apartment we shed our identities, no longer the princess and the dealer.

Just Lana and Naz.

CHAPTER SIX

Naz

THERE'S A WARM BODY CURLED into my chest when I stir awake. It's eight am, late for me as I normally rise before seven. Lana is still asleep, her small frame tucked neatly into my side, her breathing even.

I trace my fingers over her smooth, pale skin. Her skin is soft and clear, not a tattoo or flaw in sight save for the freckles that cover her cheekbones, but those are far from imperfect.

I'm beginning to think that she's flawless until I shift the sheet covering her, lowering it slightly so I can get a better view of her when my eyes are met with a dark bruise on her arm. I trace the outline of it, the dark coloring wraps around her upper arm as if someone had gripped her arm there. I think back to the night before, wondering if it was me who had bruised her.

I was rough, sure, not that she seemed to complain, but I can't imagine I marked her flesh like this.

As if sensing my concern, she stirs awake, deep hazel eyes looking up at me. "It wasn't you," she mumbles through her sleepy gaze. She closes her eyes, as if the memory of whoever bruised her is painful.

"Lana," I whisper, willing myself to muffle the anger that's rising in my chest. "Who did this?"

She turns away from me quickly, covering the offending arm. "No one," she mutters.

It's a knife to my heart.

There's a code of silence that goes hand-in-hand with this thing of ours. Even those not directly in the mafia know not to speak of it, nor speak ill of its members. As she turns from me, lifting off the bed and attempting to find her dress, dread builds in my heart.

Because I know that whoever hurt her is protected. No one would lay a hand on a *principessa* unless they knew that no harm would come to them. Like her father, or worse.

"Lana," I repeat her name, this time louder, more stern. "Just tell me. Maybe I can help you?" I'm pleading, and from the look on her face when she spins around, she knows as well as I do that neither of us can help her.

"Yeah?" she says, and there's an edge to her voice I haven't heard before. Disdain, I think. "You want to help me, Naz?" She tosses her hands up in the air. "How? What are you going to do?"

"I can talk to them," I say, but even I know how stupid that sounds.

"To whom? Marcus?"

I run a hand through my hair, fighting to think of a less stupid plan. Marcus won't care. He would marry off his own sister in a heartbeat. He doesn't give a damn about the women in his family, he only cares about power. And the alliance they're solidifying with Lana's marriage is for him as much as it is for her parents.

"Let me think!" I growl, swiping my hand across my night stand and knocking the lamp to the ground. It shatters into pieces, causing Lana to flinch.

"It doesn't matter," she says softly. "It's a done deal."

I cross the bed, my knees hitting the soft mattress as I go to her, pulling her hand and spinning her back to me. "Please," I add, "let me figure something out."

She shakes her head, dark hair spilling over her shoulders while she laughs lightly. A small hopeless

71

smile gracing her lips. "It's useless," she tells me, and at the same time I can see the fight has drained from her. She came to me last night as a last hurrah, a last fuck-you to the establishment that is the Costello *Famiglia.* But now, now that it's over, she resigned herself to the fate of her impending marriage.

The stupidity of my actions falls over me like a wave, dragging me under the surface as I realize how much I jeopardized by bringing her here, knowing her family's plan for her. I scrub a hand over my jaw as I let her go.

She's right, I can't help her.

Quietly, she picks up her discarded dress from last night, pulling it over her head and searching for her shoes. When she's dressed again, her hair tied neatly on top of her head and the wrinkled dress covering her body, she asks me for a ride home.

It feels like a block of lead is sitting at the bottom of my stomach as we leave my building, both of us walking slowly to the car, knowing that these are the final moments of a relationship that never was and never will be.

Can't be.

I slide on a pair of aviators as we slip out into the sun. She stops first, her back going rigid as she looks out to the curb where my Jeep is parked. My eyes follow hers to the figure that leans against my car, dressed in a navy blue suit and white shirt. He has a sinister lopsided smile when he sees us together.

"Hello, *fiancée*," he sneers.

CHAPTER SEVEN

Naz

THERE'S A SOUR TASTE IN my mouth as I settle into the passenger seat of Marcus' Camaro. Seeing my boss standing alongside Congressman LaFontaine outside of my loft did nothing to ease my anger this morning. After finding the bruises on Lana's arms, the last thing I wanted to do was face her abusers.

But I also knew I couldn't act on that anger. Not if I wanted to live, and I do.

The scowl etched across Marcus' face was a clear indicator, telling me I was on his shit list. He slides into the seat next to me with an annoyed scoff. Marcus is a big guy with thick muscles acquired from too many hours spent in the gym.

I knew Lana was off-limits when I brought her up

to my loft, not that she wasn't a willing participant. She loved everything I did when I had my hands on her last night. But her family, my employers, don't want NOLA royalty in the hands of scum like me.

From the front window, I watch LaFontaine man-handle Lana into his car. The look on his face is sinister but not outright angry. Instead, I can see the frown marring his tanned skin and his straightened spine as he shoves her into the SUV. On the outside, he doesn't look out of control at all, but I can see a silent rage stewing behind his eyes, and I can't imagine what he'll be like once that metal door closes and he's hidden behind the tinted windows of his Range Rover.

As much as I want to run to her aid and push the asshole off her, shove him down to the gravel and fuck up his pretty face, I know I can't. LaFontaine holds too much power in this city, and Marcus is far too loyal to him to protect me.

And I'm a nobody. A low-level street dealer. Killing me means nothing to them.

I've been running around, working for Marcus for months now trying to get my button, and one night with Lana Romano threw it all out the window.

"You're a stupid fucking kid," Marcus says, shaking his head to either side as he presses the button to start the Camaro. "You got a death wish."

Maybe.

Why else would I bring the hazel-eyed beauty home?

It wasn't like there was ever a moment when I didn't know who she was. She never lured me in under false pretenses. I was well aware of what I was doing every step of the way.

But I couldn't stop myself.

Lana Romano has me completely infatuated.

And if I don't make it past tonight, she will be the one to sign my death warrant.

"She doesn't want to marry him," I mutter as a final act of defiance.

Marcus chuckles next to me. "Doesn't matter what she wants."

My stomach clenches at his blatant disregard for her feelings. If that were my sister...

No woman deserves to be powerless next to a man, but the fact that Marcus is fine to treat his own family like that makes me sick to my stomach.

And yet he's the one with all the power here.

My family is dependent on the money I make working for Marcus. As much as my mother doesn't like to take the devil's money, as she calls it, they need it. Combined, my mom and Elly barely make anything, and they need to take care of Anthony. Every cent I earn is critical.

For a brief moment, I wonder what it would be like to be Marcus. He relies on no one but himself. His family set him up well, sure, paired with the fact that royal blood runs through his veins. But then he turned that into something, built a distribution system that turned profit. Not to mention whatever he has going on in his new strip club. He recently built a fancy club in the old red-light district. The place has been packed every time I've stopped by.

"What if that was your sister?" I ask. Marcus' little sister is barely twenty with blue hair and a wild streak.

He laughs. "I offered her up but LaFontaine has a taste that's a bit... classier."

My guts twist and I fight the urge to throw up the contents of my stomach. I guess he likes young girls, just not young girls with blue hair and an attitude. And I guess I can understand that. If you're looking for arm candy, Lana's it. She's quiet and beautiful, raised to be the perfect wife. Who wouldn't want her?

"So what?" I ask, knowing I'm on the verge of pissing off my boss and possibly getting a bullet in the back of my head. "You gonna drag her down the aisle?"

Marcus chuckles next to me. "If that's what it takes, yeah. See, you're not getting it, Naz. It's doesn't matter a single fuck what Lana wants, she can kick and scream, throw a fucking fit if she wants, but one way or another she'll walk down the fucking aisle and marry the congressman."

A shit-eating grin spreads across his cheeks. He has no shame. I don't know if Marcus even has any feelings in that thick skull of his. I let myself sink back into the leather seat of the Camaro, letting my body rest for what might be the last time.

Marcus is silent the rest of the way until he pulls up to an old building in the warehouse district. His men, big goons with too many muscles, are already waiting when we pull in. As soon as he's in the parking spot, the door is thrown open and I'm pulled from the car. My arms are pinched between the bulky hands of his men as they drag me into the warehouse.

I nearly fall, tripping over my own feet as they drag me into the warehouse. Inside is a room with thick cinder block walls that will prevent my screams from being heard. Marcus follows behind. Every few steps, I catch a glance of his mocking face over my shoulder.

It's not even like Marcus is in line to take over his grandfather's position as the head of the family, but the guy acts like he's hot shit. It grates at my nerves. I want to put the shithead in his place.

When they get me into the room, they toss me onto a metal chair. A cheap one, the kind you rent in bulk for a backyard party. They use duct tape to secure me to the metal, haphazardly stripping it from the roll and circling my limbs.

My stomach sinks every step of the way.

Damien steps in next. I recognize him from the night I met Lana. The same night her sister leaped from her balcony and Marcus dragged me there to clean up the mess. Because selling drugs isn't enough. If you want your button, want to officially join *la fa-miglia*, you have to get your hands dirty. That was the night I first soiled my hands.

I still see Lily's body when I close my eyes at night. I can see her mangled limbs, the bone that protrudes from her arm. Her blood spread over the pavement, taking two rounds of pressure washing to get the tinge of red to disappear.

I vomited as soon as I got home that night, rushing to the toilet in my mom's house and spending the next hour hunched over the bowl. Until then, I didn't realize how much I didn't want to see broken bones and bloody cracked skulls. I'd assumed my stomach was made of iron and I had no gag reflex, but I was very wrong.

Damien gives me a cold look as he slowly walks to stand in front of my chair. "So," he says thickly, "did you touch my daughter?"

Lana didn't give me the impression that she was a pure flower, she seemed eager to sink to her knees for me, but her father is making me feel like I just defiled the princess.

I'm unsure what answer is my best bet of getting out this basement. "Yes," I breathe, uttering the truth. I want to believe that these men honor truth, I would think this would be in their oath as a brotherhood. But I've worked for Marcus for a while now, and I know without a doubt that he's a liar and a cheat. So there's a chance that the truth means shit to them.

Damien bares his teeth at my answer. "Ya little fuck," he growls, winding back his fist and punching me in the face. My neck pivots from the motions, whipping my head to the side and sending a sharp pain through my skull.

I don't apologize.

I don't want to, and I'm not sorry for fucking his daughter. She's a grown woman. She chose to come home with me, to spread out on my bed and let me touch her smooth skin, let me fuck her until she begged me to stop.

The door to the cement room opens again, and through the strands of black hair that have fallen over my eyes, I can see Congressman LaFontaine enter. His brown loafers scuff the cement floor as he struts in.

I want to ask how Lana is. Mention that it didn't seem like she wanted to go with him. But I figure that's not in my best interest.

He stalks over, standing in front of me and letting his eyes scan up and down my body. So far I'm fairly unscathed, just the single black eye Damien gave me and a few sore spots from being manhandled into the chair.

I can tell he's not amused by my lack of injuries.

Apparently, he's taking me being with Lana very personal.

His face turns to Damien, looking him in the eye. "I want the bastard dead."

CHAPTER EIGHT

Lana

I'M CONVINCED THERE WILL BE a hand-shaped bruise on my other arm from the forceful way Davis grips me. With only one hand he pushes me toward the car, not caring when my body hits against the metal exterior. He shifts his gaze to either side, making sure we don't have an audience before he gives me another shove. His hand squeezes, tightening his already forceful hold as he leads me into the car, shoving me in the backseat.

I'm not going to cry.

I won't let myself be weak in front of him.

There was a quote I read once from a survivor of abuse. Something saying that only weak men hit their wives.

But Davis LaFontaine doesn't seem weak to me.

Beneath his white dress shirt, I can see the ripples

of muscles that lead down his arms and the outline of his abs. He straightens himself, slamming the back door in my face before he climbs into the front seat of his SUV.

The car is thick with tension and my breath comes out in shaky waves as I wait for Davis to say something. I'm too nervous to turn my head around and look for Naz. Marcus came to take him away, which means my parents most likely already know. My stomach clenches.

Twenty years old and I'm afraid of my parents.

Everything feels heavy, weighted down. Like there are cinder blocks tied to my ankles, the weight taking me under with them. I can't breathe under the water, can't suck in enough oxygen to keep myself alive.

I want to sink into the feeling, let the nothingness take over so I don't have to feel my heartbeat in my chest at this heightened pace.

"You're a stupid fucking girl," Davis finally says.

My breathing hitches, waiting for the next strike. The foot that will drop and destroy me, shredding my life to pieces.

"Did you enjoy your night?" Davis asks, a sinister sound to his voice.

Yes. I let the unsaid word sit between us.

Last night with Naz was everything I wanted. Everything I needed.

The walls of my mind, the mental prison I'd constructed, crumbled to pieces last night. He freed me from my obligations, from my guilt and fear. He released me from my mind, deconstructing all my fences.

I can still feel butterflies in my stomach when I think about his hands on my skin, the taste of his cock on my tongue.

"Answer me," Davis demands and I have the sick desire to tell him my internal thoughts. Let him know that he'll never make me feel the way Naz did last night. He'll never make me slick with desire; my heart will never flutter with need for him.

I will never love Davis LaFontaine.

"Yes," I say, meeting his reflection in the rearview mirror.

Anger rises in his eyes, turning them cold and mean. "Good," he says. "Because you'll never see him again, understand? That boy is as good as dead."

My heart stops beating, the blood stops pulsing through my veins. It feels like everything around me has come to a grinding halt.

Did I just kill Naz? One night of sleeping with me ends his life? Just like that?

The breath I finally pull into my lungs is loud, gasping. Davis chuckles, clearly happy with the re-action. "That's right," he sneers. "It's a hard lesson, doll, but one you need to learn. You're mine now, and I don't share well. If you ever do that again, I'll make sure what happens to your friend is worse than death. Do you understand me?"

My vision blurs, dark spots block my eyesight. I can barely take in the end of his monologue, my heart racing too fast and blood rushes through my ears.

"Lana." His voice is bitter and demanding. "Do you understand me, girl?"

"Yes," I choke out the word, the taste of it feel-ing like ash on my tongue. I'm certain that I'm going to vomit in the back of his fancy car. My stomach is convulsing, my pulse is racing. I have no control over myself. No control over my life.

I'm falling to pieces.

A sinister chuckle comes from his lips. "Good girl," he breathes. "I'd hate for you to have to learn the hard way."

My father doesn't talk to me before he leaves with Davis. An act I'm entirely grateful for. I don't think I could handle anymore yelling or scolding today.

My body is buzzing as I hike the stairs of our house, heading for Lily's room.

My mother was quick to empty most of its contents, clearing out her life as if it never existed.

Her four-post bed still sits in the center, anchoring the room with its tall white posts. The mattress is bare, nothing but a simple white cover.

I miss the color that used to saturate this room. Lily was bright and lively. She shined wherever she was, lighting up the room with her personality. Everyone loved her; she was the type of person everyone wanted to be around. Fun and goofy, nice to everyone. I admired my big sister.

Now, she's nothing. Just a pile of ash, nested inside a gold urn and hidden away in Lafayette Cemetery.

The room she left behind is empty. Cleared of all its contents so my mother doesn't have to face her mistakes. We don't talk about Lily or what happened that night. Instead, we shove all the emotions deep down and avoid ever speaking about it. I'm desperate to know what my mother feels. Does she cry at night? Does she have regrets? I can't understand how you have a child, raise them for over twenty years, and then just move on.

She jumped!

I want to scream the statement at my mother more often than I'd ever admit. Her daughter leaped from her balcony rather than talk to her. All because of this stupid marriage.

I'm starting to understand my sister better. The powerlessness that she felt. The way it crept into her bones and made her heavy, like if she jumped into the ocean she could just sink to the bottom. For the first time, I think I understand why she jumped off the balcony.

What's the point of living if it feels like this?

Like my life is not my own.

I make my way toward the balcony, letting the fresh warm air hit my skin.

My fingers trace over the edges of the iron railing. I was so jealous that she had a balcony. It pissed me off to no end that she got the good room only because she was older. I wanted this room, with its better lighting and view. The balcony I would have never used. I just wanted it because she had it.

My whole life was spent wanting to be like my big sister.

Now I imagine her lying in bed looking out here and not seeing the beauty of New Orleans, the trees behind her window, the clouds in the sky.

Instead, she saw a way out.

One jump to end it all.

Another sob wrecks from me and I fling a hand toward my chest, trying to soothe the pain that settles there. My legs shake and I sink to my knees, letting them hit the hard tile while I double over. The world feels like it's crashing down around me, everything I have crumbling to the ground.

Is this what Lilly felt? Did her heart ache and her bones turn to lead? Is this why she couldn't stand to live anymore?

Did Davis hit her? Drag her kicking and screaming?

Did he threaten her? Promise to destroy her world?

I glance over the edge of the balcony; how high could this be? Thirty? Forty feet?

Did it hurt when her body hit the pavement? Did she feel her bones snap and her skull crack?

Does it even matter in the end?

I consider for a moment throwing my leg over the iron and testing it out. Letting my body fall freely, letting everything float away as I crash to the ground.

I don't think I blame her anymore.

I think falling sounds pretty nice.

CHAPTER NINE

Naz

THE SKIN ON MY FACE throbs and every vertebrae of my neck burns as if a fire has taken the place of my bones.

I can't cry.

Not in front of these men.

"Again," LaFontaine demands, and again Damien brings his fist to my face.

Crying is a weakness, one they don't admire. Right now, they're angry, and they're using me as a punching bag, distributing their anger through rough hits. Damien is the worst of them. Bold rings adorn his fingers, and when he curls them into a fist and slams them into my face, the metal cuts the skin. He's taken to hitting the same place over and over again, the rings digging into the broken flesh.

Blood flies from my face and mouth with each hit.

I feel like a broken shell of myself.

My right eye has sealed itself shut. I don't blame it, I wish I could seal off my entire body, curl inside myself and protect my fragile bones and broken flesh.

"Again," LaFontaine says, and Damien shakes off his wrist. He winces ever so slightly. Hurting me must be taking a toll on him. He steps back and pats Marcus's shoulder. Guess he's up next.

Every inch of me *hurts*.

Pain that never felt imaginable to me. I'd been in fights before, I've held my own, but nothing compares to this.

The tape bites into my wrists, the flesh there is raw and rough.

Marcus doesn't have rings, a small blessing, but his punches are harder than his uncle's. He gives my face a break, instead, going for my stomach.

I'm thankful I didn't eat this morning, leaving me with nothing but acid to spit up.

I try to distract myself while Marcus continues the assault on my body. I bring my mind to a different place. I imagine the feeling of my ma's carpet beneath me, the shiny plastic of a PlayStation controller in my hand and Anthony laughing next to me. That kid loves video games, much to Ma's dismay. He's good too, his fingers are quick with the triggers.

Smack.

I feel the sting of Marcus's hand as it collides with my face, whipping my head to the side and jolting my neck. The fire burns down my spine again.

I need a better distraction from the pain. I let my mind wander to the last place, letting a vision of Lana fill my head. Her lipstick smeared so prettily when she took my cock in her mouth, her head bobbing up and down. Her tongue felt like velvet, washing over my cock in the most delicious ways.

The door opens again, letting in a small sliver of fluorescent light from the stairway.

"Stop." The two men who entered the basement are blurry. I have to blink a few times with my good eye before they start to come into focus. The older one has a head full of dark but graying hair and a thick mustache. He crosses his arms over his bulky chest and glances at me briefly before looking at his brother-in-law and nephew.

I don't interact with Carmine Costello Junior often. Marcus and Damien run their side of the organization separate from the man. Old Carmine had a division in his ranks, one he tried his hardest to ignore, forcing the men to gather around his dinner table and talk often. But when the old man wasn't around, things were different.

It was apparent, even to soldiers like me, that

there was a fracture between Junior and Damien. Junior was the only Costello son, but also the youngest, and for some reason his sisters' husbands felt the family was better off with them.

There's a legend, told in whispers between soldiers, when none of the Costellos are listening. Talks about how the oldest Costello girl's husband was killed. Marcus's father married Caterina Costello when they were only eighteen, much to the dismay of her father. Carmine apparently hated Marcus' father, Al Ricci. The guy was notorious for bombing buildings back in the nineties. He handled any situation he didn't like with fire. I had to admit, I kind of admired the guy, except for his psychopathic tendencies and his love for a blow torch, he stood for what he believed.

When Carmine was done with his son-in-law's antics, he gave Junior the okay to kill the man. And Junior took him out with fire, singeing off his skin until his body couldn't take anymore. Fitting, I think.

I would pass it off as talk, blown out of proportion as the years went on, but the way Marcus looks at his uncle now confirms there's bad blood there.

"What are you doing here?" Marcus asks, shaking my blood from his hand.

Behind Junior is his mini-me, Sam. He looks like

a younger version of his father, dressed in all black with a dark head of hair. His eyes are glued to me, assessing every cut and bruise decorating my skin.

Junior and Sam run one faction of the Costello *famiglia* while Damien and Marcus run the other.

How did I find myself wrapped up in a family war?

I should have known better, should have known that the stories of this family are true. That they're the brutal, uncaring monsters that the press has made them out to be.

But the money was too good.

And I'd been poor for too long. The cash lining my pockets was addicting. There was food on the table, clothes on our backs. The water was never shut off, the lights were always working. Coming home to no crisis, to no issues, was nice. There had been too many years where all we did was work, each of us holding down multiple minimum wage jobs just to keep the lights on. With this money though, Elly could be home with Anthony, and Ma could finally take a break. Age had worn out her joints, making her stiff and achy. Now she could afford a doctor, could get treatment for her arthritis.

Money opened up so many doors we hadn't even known existed.

I got greedy, taking on every job I could because I never wanted the cash flow to end.

But I guess it ends here with my blood being washed down a basement drain.

"I heard you were torturing someone," Junior answers Marcus' question, his words laced with annoyance. "Stupid, ya know," he adds, plucking a cigarette from the pack and bringing it to his lips. He doesn't finish until after he blows out the smoke. "Can this place be traced back to you?"

Marcus grinds his teeth, clearly annoyed with his uncle's statement. I'm guessing that's a yes then.

Junior shakes his head dismissively. "Enough," he speaks. "You're not killing this boy down here."

"He's my soldier," Marcus retorts.

LaFontaine leans against the cinderblock wall, watching the altercation.

"You" — Junior jabs a finger in his direction — "I've told you before that this is not your business."

The corners of LaFontaine's lips rise into a sinister smirk. "Yeah, but Damien wants the merger I offered." He shrugs his shoulders.

My stomach drops at his statement.

"I don't give a fuck," he spits back. "Sam, release the kid and make sure he doesn't talk, hear me?"

The tan boots that cover Sam's feet move toward

me, and with every step, relief floods my body. Before he gets to me, Marcus steps in his path. "No," he says, blocking Sam with an arm.

Sam chuckles, the sound is deep and throaty, scary as shit. "You don't make the decisions, *cugino*."

"This is my warehouse," Marcus responds, a whine entangled with the words.

"Don't care," Junior says, his voice angry from repeating himself.

Sam pulls a slim knife from his pocket, slicing through the tape like butter. Blood rushes to all the numb areas of my body. I rub my raw wrists, bringing the circulation back to them. Sam helps me stand up and I let him, not wanting to shrug off help from someone higher than me. "I'm okay," I choke out the words through the pain that radiates through my body. I don't want to be weak, but I also don't want to be inconsiderate.

He nods his head, letting go of me and watching as I limp off in pain.

I'm in bad shape. They mostly hit me, and my face took the bulk of the damage. Even so, my ankles are weak from where the tape bit into them and my thighs and stomach are sore. Tomorrow morning, my body will be covered in bruises, I'm sure.

Sam leads me outside. It's still bright out, but I

have no idea what time it is. We left my apartment early, but it feels like I've been in the warehouse for days.

I limp to the sleek black Audi that Sam unlocks. He opens the passenger door for me and I thank him, even though I feel embarrassed for needing the help.

My body sinks into the soft leather and I breathe a sigh of relief. I thought I was going to die in there, thought my final moments would be strapped to a chair getting the shit beat out of me.

My body shakes and I feel weak for it, desperate and pathetic.

"It's okay," Sam tells me as he slides into the driver's seat. "You're not weak for being shaken up. That's the point." He turns on the car with a press of a button and shifts into gear. "They want you to feel weak, want you to give up on life, that's how they know you'll comply."

He pulls out onto the road and I'm thankful to have the warehouse drift away into the background.

"Thank you," I whisper.

"Don't mention it." He taps his fingers against the steering wheel as he drives, letting the silence stretch between us.

Every nerve in my body is burning, the pain that drifts through me feels like the end. And yet, my family comes to the top of my mind. How the fuck am I going to support them without the money I make from Marcus. I feel a weight on my chest, crushing me again. I can't go back to part-time jobs, to heavy labor. I groan out loud, the frustration washing over me.

Sam gives me a look. "You okay?"

"I can't work for him, right?" I ask, even though I know the question is stupid.

Sam chuckles. "No. I don't think you'd want to work for Marcus, anyway. Can I ask you something?"

I nod my head. The guy saved my life today, he can ask me anything.

"Why'd you do it? I'm assuming you did, right? Sleep with Lana, I mean. Why do it? I've had lots of pussy before and I'd never risk my life for it."

"Yeah," I mutter. "It was stupid."

"So, why then?" he presses.

I don't know what to tell him. I'm not sure I know why I slept with Lana.

I saw those hazel eyes, filled with so much fucking sadness and I wanted to change them. I wanted to see an emotion in those eyes that wasn't complete and total loneliness. Maybe I saw in her the same despair that rests in me. That need, no desire, to do or be more. Searching for some sort of meaning in life. That same crushing weight of responsibility that breaks your soul and keeps you from becoming anything. I could see the fire dancing behind her eyes, just barely covered.

Her fire matched mine.

Maybe I've always liked to play with fire. Watch the flames dance along my skin, threatening to engulf me. Because if there's no meaning, no reason for this life, then why not go up in flames?

Lana is a match waiting to combust, on the edge of burning everything down.

And maybe I wanted to be there when it happened.

"I don't know," I tell Sam with a shrug.

He laughs it off. "Well, you work for me now, kid." Sam is barely a year older than me, but I don't comment on him calling me kid.

"Why?" I ask, watching as his eyebrows rise at my response. "Why would you hire me after..." I trail, looking over my body. "All this."

He brings a hand to his jaw, running his fingers along the stubble that lines his chin. "Marcus is an ass," he says. "Has been since we were kids." His dark gaze drifts over to me. "Can you be loyal, Naz?"

I'm surprised Sam Costello even knows who I am. I nod my head.

"Those assholes"—he tilts his head back in the warehouse's direction—"have a different view of how things should work. I disagree. My father disagrees, and my grandfather did too. None of us want to see Lana married to that prick."

"Then why don't you just kill them?" I ask.

"Can't kill a made man."

Made man. Something I'm not. The title given to men who enter the brotherhood of the Costello *famiglia.*

"Why did you protect me?" I ask.

Sam chuckles. "To piss them off."

It feels wrong that my life and death hang in the balance between the men in this family. That they decide my fate based on how they want someone else to feel.

I'm nothing but a pawn in their games.

"You don't want to be that, huh? Just an object used to piss someone else off?" I don't even have to respond for him to know he's right. I hate the feeling running through my head, that I'm nothing, useless. Just a piece in a fucking game. "We can change that, ya know," he adds. "You work with me, I'll get you your button, then no one will fuck with you. You want that?"

I could say no. I could say I want out and run far

away from this fucked up family. I could find work somewhere else, somewhere not Louisiana.

But then I look at Sam in his black fitted jeans and dress shirt with the sleeves rolled up. He commands the room he walks in, takes control of the situation. In a few years, he'll probably be running the show.

I want that.

I want the power that radiates from him.

I want the indestructibility that comes from being a made man.

I want Marcus to look at me and know he can't touch me.

And for some fucked up reason, I want Lana Romano.

"Yeah," I tell him. "I want that."

CHAPTER TEN

Lana

THE SMOOTH SURFACE OF THE tomb is warm to the touch and burns through my short-sleeved shirt when I lean back against it. I tip the half-filled bottle of whiskey toward my sister's resting place. "Cheers," I tell her, bringing the bottle to my lips.

Lily rests next to my grandfather. The Costello tombs are supposed to be in order of age and family, but after Lily's suicide, Grandfather had her placed next to his tomb. On the other side of his marble monument rests my grandmother, Elizabetta, who died when I was ten.

The three of them rest in blissful silence while the

rest of us suffer out here in the living world.

"Must be nice," I mutter, taking another swig from the bottle of amber liquid.

I have fond memories of my grandmother. She was slim with gray hair and thick rimmed glasses. She lived in the kitchen, loved to cook, and especially loved to feed her family. Compassion radiated from her. I remember being small and running to her when I cut my knee, right past my own mother. There was a staggering difference between my mother and her mother. My mother was more interested in what Grandpa or Uncle Junior were doing. And if she wasn't with them, she was with Aunt Caterina, gossiping in the corner with a drink in her hand.

Grandma was the complete opposite. She loved through baked goods and warm hugs. She listened with her full attention, even when I only wanted to talk about Barbie dolls. She was the first person I loved to die. It was sudden. One night I went to sleep and the next day I woke up to her being gone. Later I would learn that she was sick, but I didn't know that back then.

When my mother found me at her funeral, hiding behind a plant with tears streaming down my cheeks, she gave me a speech I would never forget. *People die, Lana. Life goes on.*

I can't say she's wrong. People do die, and life does go on. But I loved her, just like I loved my grandfather and Lily.

Maybe life goes on, but my entire world stopped spinning.

First when she died.

Then when Lilly committed suicide.

And now that Grandpapa is gone.

I don't know how much more pain my heart can take. How many more funerals can I go to? How many more black dresses can I slide onto my body, wearing to church services where I have to hold in my tears?

"I figured you'd be here." Sunlight shines in my face when I look up to the voice.

Madi chuckles softly and leans against the tomb across from Lily's. She weaves a hand through her blue hair, her act of rebellion. Her color choice was the talk of the family for an entire week. Caterina even cried about it. Dark roots span the top inch of her head, feathering out into the bright blue color. I personally think it looks cool, but I also think my mother would have a cow if I dyed my hair.

That's the difference between Madi and I, though. She doesn't succumb to the ideals that were thrust upon her. She's always made her own path in life.

It didn't hurt that she's the baby of the family and Grandfather always took her side.

"What are you doing here?" I ask, a slight stutter to my words, a sign that the half bottle of whiskey is working its magic.

She reaches out for the bottle and I hand it over so she can take a swig. Her lips twist into a grimace and she quickly gives it back to me. "Ugh," she groans. "I was looking for you." She rubs the back of her hand over her lips, wiping away the remnants of amber liquid.

"Why?" I ask. Madi is one of my few friends. I had more at one time, before Lily's death. My teenage years had been filled with colorful friendships, parties, and dating. But after Lily, parties felt off and talking to people became more painful. Eventually no one could bear to be with me, and when I finally woke up from my crippling depression, I only had a few people left. Madi was one of them.

She averts her gaze while her finger twirls a loose thread on the hem of her cut-offs. "Making sure you're okay." She shrugs. Madi doesn't do well with emotion. For six months after Lily's death, my grieving consisted of crying and staring at the ceiling silently. She didn't know what to say, so she'd just bring me a snack and sit in silence with me. It was better that way in reality, I didn't want to hear fluffy words and poems about grief. Or someone to tell me that everything happens for a reason.

I wanted to be pissed. I wanted to stew in my anger, let resentment wash over me. And then I wanted to cry my bodyweight in water while shoveling Ben and Jerry's into my mouth. I wanted to lie in bed, floating in the state between awake and asleep, my soul being tortured. Because my sister killed herself to escape life, I couldn't help but feel like I wasn't a good enough reason for her to want to live.

And Madi didn't try to stop my whirlwind of emotions. She just tagged along for the ride, making sure I knew I wasn't alone. I appreciated that more than I ever let her know.

"I'm okay," I tell her, bringing the rim of the bottle back to my lips and tipping my head back.

Drinking has become my new coping mechanism. I'm not sure what triggered it, but I found myself drawn to the warm haze the whiskey gave me.

Being numb had become a nice alternative to my daily life.

My father was not thrilled about my adventure with Naz. In fact, I had a new curfew of five pm, and I could only leave the house with an enforcer. My daily adventures took me to classes at Tulane and Lily's tomb, then straight home.

My enforcers didn't even ask anymore, just got in the car and drove me to the two places like clock-work.

Madi gives me a skeptical look. I can imagine that I, in fact, don't look 'okay,' considering I'm drink-ing in a cemetery at two pm on a Tuesday. I skipped all my classes today. Everything felt too heavy, and I didn't want to deal with sitting through lectures I didn't care about.

Instead I hid in the library, scrolling through Instagram until Tony brought me here. He's kind enough to sit out in the car, letting me be alone with Lily. Some of the men will follow me into the ceme-tery, taking their orders a little too seriously. I much prefer when they leave me alone; drinking with an audience is never fun for either of us.

She rolls her eyes. "You're allowed to be not okay, Lana."

I chuckle. "Why would I be 'not okay'?" I give her a fake smile. "Everything is perfect."

She senses my sarcasm immediately and eyes me sternly with her resting bitch face. "You know what I mean," she huffs. "It's okay if you're fucking pissed." She waves her hands as if gesturing to my life in gen-eral.

"What's your point, Mads?" I ask, annoyance tinging my words.

I wanted her to spit out whatever she was trying to say.

She blows a stream of air between her lips before continuing, "Ya know, just tell them fucking *no*."

I don't know why the defiance worked for Madi, or why I couldn't act out the ways she did. What would happen if I walked downstairs and told Damien and Carlotta Romano that I would not be marrying Davis LaFontaine. Ma would scream. Her voice was louder and higher pitched than an opera singer. Dad would firmly plant each of his hands on his hips and fix his deep brown gaze on me. After my body burned from fear, he would finally say "you think it's okay to disrespect your parents like this?" There had been too many times my parents had given the whole *I clothe and feed you* speech. At this point in my life I had the damn thing memorized.

I should just leave, but they'd never let me. I think my ma would stalk me across the country before she let me move out of New Orleans. My family is fucked up. I can't leave due to this silly notion that being born means I'm enslaved to them. But staying means I'm miserable.

At this point, I don't even know what happiness

feels like.

The emotion seems so foreign.

"What good would that do?" I mutter.

What would I even do if I left? My whole life has been my family. From a young age it was drilled into me that *family is everything*. I can't leave.

"I don't know!" Madi sighs. "But it's better than just resigning to...to this." She waves a hand at me.

I look down at my yoga pants and oversized t-shirt. I'd given up on style lately.

Since my parents locked me in my room after my outing with Naz, everything seemed pointless and the last thing I wanted to do was dress up. No matter what I did, I would still end up walking down the aisle to Davis, and once he had me, my life would no longer be my own.

Davis has every desire to control me, to force me into the mold of what he wants a wife to be.

Apparently when you have enough money and influence, you no longer have to date to find yourself a perfect woman. You can just force someone else to be her.

My stomach rolls just thinking about my future husband. He elicits a deep sickness in me, one that can only be cured with another swig of Jack Daniels.

"It doesn't matter," I murmur. "It would be a

waste of time to try and fight them."

Madi stares at me, her face twisted with annoyance. "So you'll just marry him?"

"Yep," I tell her, taking another chug.

My fate is sealed.

Tony drives me home from the cemetery in deafening
silence. The man doesn't speak much, and it's a fact
that makes him one of my favorite enforcers. I often
wonder how he feels about being put on "Lana duty."
He's six feet of pure muscle, like all the enforcers that
work for my father. The men with brains rarely end
up driving daughters around.

No, those men are probably off doing something
else. Inky black tattoos sprawling over olive skin
floats to the top of my mind. I can see Naz's dark
eyes, the way his fingers trace over the St. Jude metal
that falls from his throat. I wonder if he's one of the
smart ones. What kind of job does a man like Naz do
for Marcus and my father?

I let the possibilities run through my mind. My
knowledge of the American mafia comes more from
documentaries and repeats of The Sopranos rather
than my own family. My parents were quick to hide
the realities of their life from Lily and I. We always

knew something was off, as soon as we got to school it was apparent that not everyone was followed around by muscled men in black with guns strapped to their hips.

We knew our family was different.

By my teenage years, I had heard all the stories about my grandfather. To me, Papa was a hero. I love him more than I loved any other family member. He was my number one supporter, constantly amazed by everything I did. When I spoke, he listened intently, in a way that my parents never did. The version of him built up in my mind was nothing like the one in the stories I heard.

My classmates spoke of Carmine Costello as a ruthless murderer. The list of men killed on his orders was endless. Everyone I knew had a connection. People either loved him or hated him, there was no in between.

But I never saw that side of my family.

It wasn't until I Googled his name in seventh grade that I finally realized how real the rumors were. My grandfather was head of the New Orleans mafia. My father had his own Wikipedia page, citing him as a well-known Capo, a high-ranking member of the mob.

My reality shattered that day. I had been living in

an illusion, believing that my family was "normal" but all along we were criminals living a facade.

When I told Lily about my new discovery, she told me to keep it a secret, not to let Mom and Dad know that I found out. She told me it was easier that way.

But the second I saw my father, I started to cry, and he knew immediately.

It wasn't him who consoled me, though. Instead, Grandpapa came and picked me up to go out for ice cream.

We sat outside, the NOLA heat making sweat run down my cheeks while we licked the sweet sugary substance from cones. Finally, he told me that life wasn't black and white. There's no good and bad. He didn't talk down to me when he said the words, not in the way my father did when he spoke to me. My grandfather treated me like an adult.

"How did reading that article make you feel?" he asked.

No one ever asked me how I felt in my house. The Romano family was all about suppressing your emotions and putting on a good act. The better of an act we put on, the happier my parents would be.

"Bad," I had said.

We talked about that feeling for longer than anyone ever had a conversation with me, and at the end, he looked me in the eye and said *family is everything.* It was a motto he had preached since he came over to the States from Sicily with nothing but the clothes on his back. It wasn't often that he spoke of his life before I was born, so I was entranced when he finally did that day.

"There are times in life where you'll have to fight to get what you deserve, bambina. But you never fight with family, okay? I always wanted a family, a big family like this." He takes a lick of his ice cream cone. *"People who are loyal to each other, who protect each other. Family is everything, Lana."*

I internalized those words. Even when I was angry, even when my parents made me want to scream, I remember, *family is everything.*

As I walk through the front door of our home, no one greets me. There's no shout to welcome me home. No one asks me how my day was.

I miss my grandfather in this moment. Grief settles in my bones, weighing me down, making me so heavy that every step feels like I'm dragging my legs. I want to collapse on the staircase and just give up.

My heart aches and my bones hurt, and I no longer want to live like this.

"Get changed." My mother's voice sneaks up on me when she finds me slowly ascending the stairs.

ALLIANCE
"Your fiancé is coming over for dinner."

CHAPTER ELEVEN

Lana

THE WHISKEY HAS SETTLED IN my stomach. It feels like a brick of lead covered in a sticky maple syrup. It's weighing my core down and the sickly-sweet taste has left me feeling like I might vomit.

My mother, as usual, doesn't care about my current state.

When she smelled the whiskey on my breath, she told me to brush my teeth, then threw the dress she wanted me to wear on the bed, and left.

Sometimes I wonder what it's like to not love your children. To only see them as a bargaining chip. Once, when Aunt Caterina was drunk, a state not uncommon for her, she spilled my mother's secret to Madi. She never wanted kids. Carlotta Romano didn't have a maternal bone in her body, but bearing children was expected of her. She would have stopped at one, but my father wanted a boy, so they tried again. After two girls, she said no more.

Even with that knowledge, I still didn't understand.

Hollywood movies have trained me to believe that as soon as a mother holds her baby, she falls in love. How many stories had I watched where a mother held that crinkly-skinned newborn in her arms, sweat dripping down her forehead, dizzy from the epidural, but the second that child hit her chest, love bloomed? Love was the solution to every problem, as least in the movies.

I wonder how my mother reacted when they put my small body on her chest. Knowing her disdain for messes, I bet she handed me right back and asked someone to bathe me.

My heart aches at the thought.

I swish some mouthwash around in my mouth, thinking about swallowing it down and hoping the alcohol is enough to keep me buzzed. The alcohol is the only thing that helps anymore. I wake up longing for the sweet relief that comes with a swig of whiskey. I need the edges dulled, need my thoughts to slow down. Whiskey is the only thing that keeps the panic at bay.

The thought of seeing my finance makes my stomach churn. The bruises he left on my arms have only just started to disappear. Instinctively, I trace my fingers along the yellow edges.

The dress my mother left out is long sleeved; she's fully aware of the bruises that mark my skin so I'm sure she picked the dress on purpose. It hurts when I think about her actively choosing a dress to hide the marks he left on me, the man she's forcing me to marry.

I toss the silk material to the floor and head for my closet, flipping through the rack of clothes. I settle on an emerald green shift dress made of a smooth satin material. It has a delicate neckline and thin spaghetti straps. I slide the soft material over my body and let it fall. The dress does nothing to hide the faint bruises on each of my arms. He left new ones the day he found me with Naz and manhandled me into his car.

A laugh escapes my lips when I look at myself in the mirror.

The girl in its reflection looks like shit.

Bags line her eyes, and the bruises stand out on her arms. The dress is pretty, but it swallows me. I've lost weight since I've last worn it, apparently my whiskey diet has made me thin. My legs look pale and small, and my hair looks dull as I twist it back into a low bun.

I look like a sad excuse for myself, but I don't care. I don't want to look good for Davis. If he's so determined to marry me, he should know that this is what he's getting.

I'm damaged goods. Depressed and pathetic with a slight drinking problem.

If he wanted a pretty wife, he should have looked elsewhere.

"Lana!" my mother calls from downstairs, her voice high pitched and already filled with annoyance. That's all I am to her, another problem, another issue she needs to handle.

I take my sweet time heading for the stairs, not really caring how much of a rush she's in.

The liquor has given me a false sense of bravery.

Davis is standing at the bottom of the stairs, his hands tucked into his pockets while he listens to my mother drone on. In another life, I might find him handsome. With his honey-colored hair and southern drawl, he has a charming look playing around.

But I know underneath that suit and pretty face, there's a monster lurking in the shadows.

As if on cue, my arms throb. The marks he left on me haven't hurt in days, but it's like my body knows he's here and is protesting. The ache in my heart prac-tically screams at me. *Run, stupid. Why are you walking toward a predator?*

And that's what Davis LaFontaine is.

A predator.

No matter how nice his clothes are or how charm-ing he appears, that man is bad news.

He looks disappointed when he sees me coming down the stairs. His bold eyes rake over me, taking in the faint marks on my arms, my messy hair, and bare feet. Dark eyes stare into mine and I think he's looking for something, some sign that I'm not about to throw myself over the balcony railing.

If only he knew how badly I wanted to.

I don't know why I couldn't do it. I tried to swing my legs over the metal, tried to find a sick sense of satisfaction in killing myself the same way Lily did. But I couldn't do it. My legs stayed glued to the pa-tio until I finally collapsed onto the tiled surface and cried.

Even with the desire to die flooding my system, I couldn't do it.

I was weak.

"Lana," Davis says, his voice softer than I've ever heard it.

My mother scowls when she sees me, her face

twisting as if seeing me in this dress is actually painful. "What happened to the outfit I put out for you?" she questions, trying and failing to hide the anger in her tone.

I shrug. "I wanted to wear this, it lets my arms breathe."

Davis' lips pull into a straight line at my words. Clearly they hit a nerve. I feel proud of myself for the small jab. A new version of Lana has stepped forward, drunk Lana, and she doesn't cower. Or maybe it's just that she doesn't care anymore. I've run out of fucks to give.

I move past my fiancé and my mother, heading toward our formal dining room.

"Carlotta." I hear Davis' smooth voice as he turns to my mother. "Can I have a second alone with your daughter?"

"Sure." I don't turn around to watch my mother leave, instead I keep moving forward. "I'll be in the kitchen," she tells him. "Damien should be home shortly."

Before she's even gone into the kitchen, I can feel Davis stalking toward me. He feels like an invisible weight, his presence looming over me. His fingers wrap around my arm to stall my movement.

I'm weak when it comes to Davis. Can't seem to

hold on my own as he squeezes my arm in his hand and drags me back to him.

Tears burn at the edges of my eyes, but I refuse to cry for this monster. He spins me around and grips both of my arms, forcing me to face him.

"You look like shit," he growls.

"Thanks," I mutter.

"What the fuck is wrong with you? Hmm? You need to take care of yourself, and if you can't do that, I'll send someone over here to do it. Do you need to be force-fed, Lana?" He looks delighted while he berates me. I think he gets off on demeaning me.

"When you saw her…" I can't help the words that rush from my lips, the question that's on the tip of my tongue. "You said *that's a shame,* but you didn't care."

His eyes zone in on mine, his brows knitting together with a look of confusion. "What are you talking about?"

"Lily," I say, my voice cracking as her name leaves my lips. "My sister. When you saw her, you said *that's a shame.* Why?"

He drops his grip on me, letting my arms go limp at my sides. "You've been drinking," he says. "Are you even of age?"

"Apparently I'm old enough to get married, so why not drink whiskey while I'm at it?"

He scoffs, unimpressed with my answer. "You need to sober up."

"You didn't answer my question." I can tell I'm drunk, or at least very tipsy, because sober Lana would never be this bold.

Two dark eyes find me again, their stare intense. He makes me feel small as he looks down at me. "I did care," he says. "Your sister fucked up my plans and I had to wait three years for you. So, I do care, Lana dear, just not for the reasons you want me to."

The words feel like a knife to my chest. How could someone be so cruel?

"What did you say to her?"

"Lana, I don't have time to play twenty questions with you. Go upstairs and fix yourself, understand?" He gives me a shove back toward the stairs, but my feet are unstable, and I trip over myself. I can feel myself falling, but I'm useless. My hands extend, but my brain is too dizzy to find something to latch on to. My head hits the corner of the hallway table and my body bounces back before hitting the tiled floor of the hallway.

The flooring is cold against my skin. My dress flies up when I fall, and my body lays limp on the floor. I can feel something warm and wet start to run down my forehead. Groggily, I bring my hand to my face, pulling it away to see the sticky red blood coating my fingertips.

"Jesus Christ," I hear Davis mutter, and then a door swings open.

"Tell me," I mutter, my voice comes out soft and broken sounding. "Tell me."

"What happened?" It's my father's voice that booms through the hallway, and his hands that find me first.

"She's drunk, Damien," Davis says, annoyance tinging his words.

"Lana?" My dad brings a hand to my face, smoothing back my hair and meeting my eyes. For a moment, I'm convinced he cares. I can pretend that he's taking care of me, comforting me, shielding me from the abuse. But even drunk, I know that's not what's happening. I'm a commodity. An object for him to trade.

And I'm worthless if I'm broken.

I hear my mother scream, dropping a plate when she comes out of the kitchen. "What happened?" she asks, that seems to be the burning question.

If I tell them Davis pushed me, will they kick him out?

"Your daughter is a drunk." Davis hovers over me.

"Davis," my father drawls. "I can take care of this."

"You better," he growls down at my father. "She can't act like this anymore."

"Like what?" I ask. My head is throbbing, and I have no desire to get up from the icy floor. I close my eyes, dragging a long breath in through my lips.

Davis leans down, bending at the waist so he can bring his face closer to mine. "Like a bratty little child," he says. "Time to grow up, Lana,"

He rises and steps over me, nearly crushing my hair with his shiny loafer.

"Fuck you," I yell, this time louder, bolder. He freezes, then spins to look at me again.

"Yeah?"

I push myself up so I'm sitting, but he's still hovering over me, using his larger body to intimidate me.

"Are you sure you want to play this game, little girl? Do you want to see how miserable I can make you?" Spittle flies from his lips, landing on my face while he taunts me. "Or maybe…" A sinister smile rises on his face. "Maybe I should go pick up your little boyfriend. Do you think he should pay for your mistakes today?"

I haven't seen Naz since that day, though, he visits my thoughts daily. I can't get the vision of his inked body out of my head, can't stop hearing his breathy moans as I kneeled before him.

I shouldn't be bothered by the threat; I don't even know Naz.

But I am.

I don't want him to be hurt simply because Davis wants to control me. I lower my gaze and Davis chuckles, taking it as a sign that he's won this conversation.

He wipes his hand across his mouth and straightens out his jacket. "I think I'll pass on dinner tonight," he says in his perfected politician voice. "I think you have some shit to handle here."

He spins on the heel of his loafer and leaves before any of us can respond. The second the door closes, I'm met with the two angry faces of my parents, and for the last time today, I'm reminded how alone I am.

That the only people who cared about me are dead.

CHAPTER TWELVE

Naz

I SUCK IN A BREATH when I enter Ma's house, letting myself in as normal. "I'm here," I yell out, not that the house is large enough to yell.

"In here," she calls back, her voice coming from the kitchen. I'd argue that my mother's favorite room is the kitchen, every time I visit she's standing over the stove stirring a pot of something or the other.

My heart races as I head for the closed-in room behind the main living space. Ma's house is old, never to have the open floor plan that newer houses boast. I've offered to fund a renovation, but Ma's already pissy about taking my money to cover living expenses, she has no interest in using it to spoil herself. Even when I try to phrase it as an investment, something to make the house worth more whenever she wants to sell it, she dismisses me with a wave of her hand.

She'll use the money to keep the lights on, but she won't pretend to like what I do.

We've reached a kind of stalemate, where neither of us talk about my chosen profession. Instead, I drop the cash on the table. She takes it, and neither of us talk about what I did to get it.

My chest tightens as I enter the kitchen, anxiety rolling through my stomach. It's been a week since I fucked Lana, since her family beat the shit out of me in Marcus' warehouse. I avoided my family as well as I could, claiming I had the stomach flu and hiding in my apartment. Elly dropped soup off at my door, finally leaving it on the mat after I didn't answer her fifteen minutes of pounding.

I couldn't let them see me like that. Even now, my stomach clenches at the thought of my ma seeing the faded bruises and half-healed cuts.

This is what she's been afraid of, and seeing me like this will only make that fear real.

I can't blame her. I can't shrug off her fear and pretend that it will never happen, something I've done in the past. She's fifty-five years old and lived in New Orleans her entire life. Each of her friends has a story about *La Cosa Nostra*, handfuls of them have lost their sons to this organization. There was a time when she went to funeral after funeral to mourn the men that had been killed for doing exactly what I'm doing.

Because it's not the Costellos who get buried six feet under when something goes wrong on the streets. When another organization creeps their way in or when the siblings fight.

It's us.

The soldiers.

The kids who grew up on these streets begging for scraps. We get sucked into the life with the promise of cash and spit back out with bullet holes riddling our bodies.

"I brought you flowers," I say, my words sound meek and scared. I've reverted back to being a kid who fears his mother.

She's in front of the stove, steam rising from the boiling pot and rolling over her face. When she turns, she pulls the fogged glasses from her face, wiping them on her shirt before she finally slides them back up her nose and sees me. Immediately, her irises widen, the pupils huge as they skate over my face, lingering on each of the many healing cuts.

The rings on Damien's fingers left gashes on my skull. Head wounds bleed like a bitch and by the time Sam had gotten me back to my apartment, I was woozy. What she can't see is the green and yellow bruises that cover my stomach. Even after a week, I wince when I sit and stand. Too much movement leaves me feeling sore and useless.

I've spent the past seven days laying on my back while my head recounted the moments that had gotten me there.

As my new boss, Sam told me to take a week to rest and let things calm down before he would put me to work. I was thankful for the break, but also anxious. Every second I sat alone in my apartment, my cut-up face looking back at me, was a second I wanted to run. Get the hell out of NOLA and never look back.

But then what?

Do you just run away from the mob? If Sam isn't protecting me, will Marcus or Davis come after me? Davis doesn't love Lana, I'm sure of it, but he sees her as a possession and the look on his face made it clear to me that he didn't want anyone else to touch what he deemed his.

And then Lana.

I couldn't get her hazel eyes out of my head. She danced through my thoughts like a fucking ballerina, making me crazy. Would I be thinking of her like this if she wasn't off-limits? Was it the thrill of being with her I was addicted to? Or was it her?

"What happened?" Ma asks, her voice stern but fearful.

"I'm fine," I say, shrugging, trying to act like my entire body doesn't ache.

She wipes her hand on a dish towel before tossing it onto the counter and walking toward me slowly. "You're hurt," she says, the words leaving her lips in a hushed whisper. "Ignazio, who did this to you?"

"I'm fine," I repeat. I can't tell my mother that her worst fear almost came true. That she was a few minutes away from having a closed casket funeral. Or worse, an empty casket. The thought that she'd never see my body, never have closure, eats away at me.

Her brown eyes rim with water as she brings a wrinkled hand to my cheek. I lean into her touch, closing my eyes and letting her warmth permeate my skin. Even as an adult, I find comfort in my mother's touch. She's possibly the only person in this world who loves me unconditionally.

"Grammy!" I blink my eyes open when I hear Anthony's shout behind me. "Grammy! Look what Mama got me!" He stops dead in his tracks, holding a sealed PlayStation game when he sees me. "Uncle Naz…" He trails softly. "What happened to your face?"

Elly is on his heels. She turns into the kitchen and her eyes widen when she sees me. "Jesus, Naz. What the fuck happened to you?"

"Elly!" my mother scolds, but she just shrugs her shoulders. "Anthony, why don't you go play that new game, hmm? Uncle Naz will be right out."

To his credit, Anthony nods, spins on his heel, and heads out to the living room.

Ma brings each of her hands to her hips, her eyes still scanning over me, looking for more cuts, finding the bruises that peek out from under my collar.

"Ignazio, tell me what happened?"

The tone of her voice has guilt gnawing at me. "It was a misunderstanding, Ma."

Next to me, Elly scoffs. "What was the misunderstanding, Naz? Did they accidentally hit your face with their fists?" She leans back against the counter as she poses the question. Her tone is cold, but I can hear the fear that's laced into her words.

Elly's been my counterpart since we were kids. As much as we fight and torture each other, she's always been on my side. When she got pregnant at seventeen, I was the first one she told. We both knew that the boy she had been with would never take responsibility, and he proved our theory true.

So I stepped up. Working two part-time jobs to

earn enough before I found Marcus and started dealing. I know she would never admit, but she cares for me. If I ended up dead, I don't know what she'd do.

Sighing heavily, I run my fingers through my hair. "I'm sorry," I mumble. "I wasn't careful. But I'm okay, I'm alive, and I won't let it happen again."

My mother huffs, clearly not convinced with my apology. "Ignazio," she breathes, taking another step forward. She places each of her hands on my shoulders, squeezing them in that way that only mothers do. "If anything happened to you..." She trails off. "I don't know what I would do."

"I know, Ma. I'm sorry."

"You need to get out. It's not safe," Elly adds, her arms still firmly placed across her chest.

"That's not how it works, Elle, I can't just hand in my two-week resignation."

"Why?" she huffs, throwing her hands up dramatically.

"It's the mafia!" I hiss before I can think better of it. Ma retracts her hands, wrapping them around her torso like she needs to hold herself. Elly's face turns to pure shock beside me. "I'm sorry," I mutter.

Without a word, my mother turns away, dusting her hands on her apron and going back to the stove. Elly rolls her eyes. "I'm serious, Naz," she says. "You

135

need to get out before they do something worse than a few cuts."

If only she knew. It's more than a few cuts, it's an ache that radiates through my entire body. I wake up sweating through my sheets at night, thinking about the punches raining down on me, the harsh words thrown at me, the fear of almost dying pulsing through my body. I thought I was going to be killed in that basement. I know that it could have been worse.

And still, I know I won't quit.

Anthony is quiet when I sit down next to him on the pale beige carpet. His fingers grip the PlayStation controller, his eyes glued to the TV.

Normally, hanging with the kid is effortless for me, but today my heart aches and my body's sore.

"Ma sounds mad," he says, his thumbs wiggling the triggers while he shoots at someone on the screen.

"She is." I sigh, running a hand through my hair.

"What did you do?" he asks, his eyes not moving from the screen. I'm always amused by the kid's ability to simultaneously have a conversation with me, and keep moving and shooting on his game.

"It's complicated," I tell him.

Anthony only shrugs. "Sometimes, when she's

mad, I'll give her a hug and tell her I'm sorry. Did you try that?"

It sounds so simple when the kid says it. An apology should fix everything, set everything right in the world. That's what we taught him, right? I can't even remember all the times I've made the kid apologize in his eight years of life. Respect, humility, all the traits we wanted the kid to have. And he does. My heart swells at how sweet he is.

But he's also naïve.

And maybe that's because we made him that way.

We told him to be honest, to admit when he's wrong, and to hurt no one.

But where will those traits actually get him? Zipped up in a body bag or at the bottom of the ocean? My throat constricts at the thought. At what point do we all go from being naïve little kids to selling drugs on the street corners? When does it all change?

"I haven't tried that," I tell him, sucking in a breath and willing myself not to cry in front of my nephew.

"You should," he tells me in a matter-of-fact way. "You should always say you're sorry, Uncle Naz," he scolds me with a phrase I'm sure he's heard from me a million times.

"I know, buddy," I whisper. "That's good advice."

But sorry isn't going to fix this one. I don't get to

CHAPTER THIRTEEN

Naz

THERE'S NO REASON FOR ME to be in bed at eight pm on a Saturday. Except, I haven't started working for Sam yet and I'm not dealing for Marcus. So I'm jobless and purposeless.

The money that selling drugs made me bought this whole apartment. My own renovated studio. Having a place of my own felt like such an accomplishment. I was no longer slum from the West side; I felt like fucking royalty.

Now these four walls feel like a prison.

I'm trapped inside the brick, waiting for someone to tell me it's okay to leave. Waiting for the scabs marking my skin to heal. Just… waiting.

It feels like an anvil is sitting on my chest, pushing me down onto the bed and not letting me move. My breathing is shallow, lungs too compressed to suck in enough air.

But there's nothing I can do, nothing will change my current situation.

So I bear it.

At first, I ignore the sudden knock on my door. I'm too deep in my spiral to get up, anyway. But it doesn't stop. It's probably Elly, pounding relentlessly so she can come in here and scold me.

It takes effort to pull myself out of the bed, leaving the warmth of my mattress and comforter behind. I trudge to the door, scrapping my bare feet along the hardwoods.

"What?" I ask, swinging it open.

Except it's not Elly there. Instead, I come face to face with Lana. Her hazel eyes are dark as they scan my body, lingering on the waist of my gray sweatpants for too long. Her hair is swept up into a messy bun and her face is bare of makeup. She wears leggings and a big t-shirt with a pair of canvas shoes covering her feet. A bottle of Jack Daniels dangles from her fingertips.

"Are you going to let me in?" she asks, lifting the

bottle in a gesture of *I brought whiskey to solve all our problems.*

My brain shouts *no, you stupid fuck.* But my hand pulls open the door wider, and she steps through the threshold.

This is stupid.

This is how I end up with a bullet in my skull.

But how do I push her away? What words would I use to tell her no? That I'm too scared of her family to provide her any comfort?

She uncaps the bottle, tossing the metal to my counter and bringing the amber liquid to her lips. I give her credit, she swallows the whiskey down without even wincing.

"I wasn't sure..." She trails off, her gaze avoiding me. "I thought maybe..."

"Almost," I tell her, knowing exactly where her line of thought is going. She wasn't sure if I was alive or if her family killed me.

Her eyes find me now and she leans against the island in my kitchen. I keep my distance, staying by the door. I don't want to get too close to her, I can't get sucked into her orbit again.

Lana could be the fucking sun, and I would just revolve around her like a planet, lost in her trajectory, forever focused on her.

So I can't get close, because I have other people I need to be here for, and if I lose myself to her, I won't live long enough to be there for my family.

"Your face." My fingertips ache to reach out to the cut that marks her forehead, the angry red line staring at me. "Did he do that?"

The bottle comes back to her lips and she takes another gulp before she meets my gaze again. I know instantly, before she says the word, that I'm right. The man is a harsh asshole, clearly not above abuse.

Her eyes scan over the pale cuts that linger on my face, down to my arms where she finds the bruises that peek out of the sleeves of my black t-shirt.

She brings the bottle to her lips, taking another long gulp. "What did they do to you?" she asks, her voice barely above a whisper.

"Lana..." I trail. "You don't want to know." We're a sad pair, I think, both standing in my kitchen with a bottle of whiskey trading war stories and admiring each other's cuts. How fucked up is that?

"I do," she says, her response is so quick. "I need to know. I need to know what they did to you. It's my—"

My legs take me to her in two quick steps, before I can even acknowledge what I'm doing. My hands find her shoulder, gripping them tightly and forcing her to look at me. "It's not your fault," I tell her stern-ly. "You didn't do a damn thing to me. They did. And you can't sit here and believe that their actions have anything to do with you."

Those hazel eyes stare into mine. There's a storm brewing behind them, I can see the twisting emo-tions, the grief that lingers there. I practically feel it, her storm radiates from her, covering me in her anger and grief.

I take the bottle from her hands, tipping it back and taking a chug of the whiskey. I don't know how to be near her without losing myself. Sadness hangs from her, everything about her screams *I'm fucking depressed*. I can see it in the shadows that rest under her eyes and in the water that pools on her lash line. I can see how the stress has morphed her smile, giving her frown lines. She looks at me like she's treading water, grasping for anything to keep her above the surface.

But I know if I give her my hand, I'll go under with her.

Maybe that's all she wants, just for someone to drown with her.

I take another swig of the liquor, hoping for some kind of strength. But I know all I'll find in this bottle is weakness. And fuck, if I'm not about to be weak with her.

"What are you doing here, Lana?" I ask, shoving the bottle of Jack back to her.

Her lips twitch, the movement so subtle, but I notice it. I can see how the corners perk up when she looks at me, like she sees something, and it makes her smile. Goddamn it, if I don't want to see that smile.

Fuck, I think I would burn down this apartment if it made her smile again.

My hand lifts and my thumb finds the corner of her lip, gently skimming across the smooth surface. How is it even possible for her to feel like this? For her skin to be so silky and perfect? I want to run my fingers along every inch of her, committing every detail to memory.

I need her to leave.

I need her out of my apartment before I do something stupid.

"I needed to know," she tells me. "I needed to see if you were okay."

"Don't worry about me. I can handle myself."

There it is. That twitch again. That threat of a smile trying to fight its way to the surface.

"All I do is worry, Naz," she says. "I worry about everything and everyone. I can't fucking stop. It's all I can think about."

We're silent for a moment, our eyes staring into one another, our bodies far too close. Everything inside me screams, telling me to run, to get the fuck away from this girl.

"Lana," I whisper.

"I need you to make me forget," she says before I can even get another word out. "I need to forget about everything, and I think you're the only one who can help me."

"Lana," I try again, searching for some logic to come to the top of my brain. Some excuse to kick her out.

"Please," she whispers, and my heart crumbles inside my chest, turning to fucking dust. "Please, Naz, help me forget."

My lips crash into hers with too much force, but she doesn't care. She meets me there, her tongue warring with me, her hands reaching up to run through my hair.

I feel frantic in my need for her. I can't kiss her enough; my hands can't get a good enough feel of her. It's like she's slipping away, even though she's right here. I need to savor every second that I have my hands on her, but I also can't move fast enough.

My chest is pounding, my heart aching with need.

I don't even feel the stiffness in my body, the ache

in my muscles as I lift her up, letting her ass hit my countertop.

I grip the elastic of her leggings, dragging the tight material down her thighs. I want to taste her, but I *need* to feel her. I can't move fast enough, dragging my sweats down my legs, taking my boxers with them and tossing both to the side with her leggings.

Her hands grip onto my shoulders, her nails biting into me even through the cotton t-shirt. I drag a finger through her slit, finding her already wet for me.

"Please," she begs, and the sound rings through my ears like a beautiful fucking melody.

I don't make her wait, instead, I bring the head of my cock to her pussy, coating it with her wetness before I slide in. She moans, the sound so fucking beautiful as I thrust into her.

I can't get enough. The sounds she makes, the way she feels when the walls of her pussy clench around my cock.

This isn't the same as the last time I had her in this room. If feels more frantic, more final. Like this might be the last time I ever see her, or the last time either of us live to be together.

My body is buzzing, a new found energy running through me. I'm addicted to this woman, to her soft skin and sweet smile. I'm attracted to her pain, wanting to cover her and protect her.

I want to worship her body, create a church dedicated to the angel that's fucking me.

I want to bow down and pray to this beautiful woman every day.

But I know that once we finish, she'll walk out that door and I'll never see her again.

And that's the way it has to be.

I thrust into her harder, listening to the soft cries that leave her lips. "Naz," she pants. "I'm so close." Her voice is breathless, her words coming out in a husky whine.

I bring my finger to her core, dragging her juices to her clit and rubbing circles around the bundle of nerves. Her eyes squeeze shut, her breath coming out in short pants.

"Look at me," I demand. "Fucking look at me, Lana. I want you to see only me when you cum. I want you to remember this, remember the way you cry for my cock, the way your pussy grips on to me like you've never been fucked this good. Am I the best fuck you've ever had?"

She doesn't answer, instead she heaves a breath, and I can feel her tightening around me, so goddamn close.

"Tell me," I demand. "Tell me, baby. Has anyone ever fucked you like me?"

"No," she breathes out. "No one's ever fucked me this good." She barely has the words out before she crashes over the edge of her orgasm. Her eyes close so tightly and her breath comes out in harsh pants.

The sight of her coming undone around my cock is enough to push me over to the edge to my own release. I pull out just in time, gripping my cock in a tight vise while I let the ropes of my cum paint her legs like a beautiful fucking canvas.

We're both panting, gripping onto each other and the countertop. Her hazel eyes find mine and she doesn't have to say a word for me to know exactly what she's thinking. I can't let her go, even though I know I need to. Even though I need to walk away, protect myself, and my family. Even though I can still feel the bruises, the aches in my body from the last time I fucked up.

And still, even with all of that, I can't let her go that easily.

I think she might be worth saving.

Or dying for.

CHAPTER FOURTEEN

Lana

THE HOUSE FEELS SAD AND empty.

One week until Christmas, and even though we have a tree and decorations, our house feels anything but festive.

My parents watch me constantly. Their eyes find me no matter what room I go to, following me around like they're waiting for me to fuck up. Since Davis' show in our entryway, no one trusts me. All the liquor bottles have been moved and locked away. It seems that Davis' comment about me being a drunk has been taken to heart.

I never really drank; I never enjoyed the taste of it despite Lily dragging me to parties constantly. Even after her death, I wasn't drawn to the numbing sensation. But Grandpa's death paired with my engagement was more than I can take.

The depression has paired perfectly with the swell of my anxiety. The two haven't let me fully sleep, instead keeping me locked inside the prison of my head. Unable to rest, constantly overtaken with the swirling, endless thoughts.

The alcohol soothes the ache that is my brain. Placing a nice haze over the surface, keeping the thoughts from moving too fast. Instead, they're sluggish, slowly trailing through the fog.

It's the only time I can breathe. The only time I can lay my head back and calm the fuck down.

Every second of the day my brain is racing, for what I have no idea, but once the whiskey slides down my throat, I can take a breath.

I miss it already.

There's a pale, white lace dress hanging on my closet door. The sight of which is overwhelming. If I have a panic attack over the dress for my engagement party, how the fuck am I going to walk down the aisle?

I haven't seen Davis since that day in the entryway. My stomach convulses at the thought of seeing him tonight. I don't think I can handle feeling his touch on my skin. Or faking that I'm not repulsed by him.

I breathe in, letting the air fill my lungs before I blow it through my lips. There are no options here, I have to make it through tonight. I have to put on a brave face, even though every fiber of my being is screaming not to.

But could I even get out of this? Even if I ran, if I abandoned my parents, then what? Where would I go, what would I do? I have nothing that is my own. Everything is tied to the Costello name, and while I want to say I would give it all up, I don't know how to live without it. I've never even lived in a different house. Every year of my life has been spent in this room.

I feel like one of those spoiled rich kids that everyone sneers at.

But I don't feel privileged in my heart.

Caged.

That's how I would describe this feeling.

"Lana." My mother's fist hits against my door while she calls my name.

I don't want to move from my spot on my bed. The idea of having to get up, see people, and talk makes my body ache. I groan in protest, rolling onto my side and facing away from the bedroom door.

My mother doesn't wait to be invited in, instead

she flings the door open and enters my room. I can't see her face, but I'm sure it's twisted in disgust as she peers around.

I haven't left my room in nearly twenty-four hours. Most of that time has been spent in this bed, squirreled away under the covers trying to hide from everything.

Carlotta doesn't get that, though. She expects me to straighten my shoulders and do as I'm told, like I'm a robot and not a human being.

"Lana," she says again. "You need to shower. Start getting ready. We need to leave in an hour," she huffs. I'm sure she's fully dressed. She spends hours getting ready, perfecting her look. My mother is a vain character. She runs on complaints and envy, the kind of superficial woman you only see in movies.

As much as I don't want to leave my bed, I can't stand listening to my mother yap about getting ready and impressing people. So I roll from my blanket co-coon and head to my en suite bathroom.

She leaves me alone eventually after shouting how she wanted my hair done. I spend too much time in the shower, letting the scalding water burn my skin, praying the spray would melt me and wash me down the drain.

But I'm still here.

I spend less time on my makeup than I'm sure my mother hoped for, but I still look like a perfectly made mafia princess. I line my eyes with black, sharp wings jutting from the corners. My cheeks are a flushed pale pink, and a subtle rose color is applied to my lips. I heat up the curling wand, putting some loose spirals in my hair.

Finally, I grab the lace dress, pulling the white fabric over my head and zipping it up the side. I slip my feet into the soft pink heels and stare at myself in the mirror.

I don't like the girl who looks back at me.

She looks too prim and proper. Too virginal and innocent.

She looks nothing like me.

But underneath, I know she's broken. I feel the ache in my chest, the racing thoughts in my head. I want everything to stop, but I don't know how to get out of this.

My heart races as I head for the stairs, but my fingers shake as I grip the railing.

I'm not ready.

I don't think I'll ever be ready to see Davis LaFontaine.

Davis is already at the restaurant when we arrive. Dressed in a dark navy suit with a white linen shirt. He looks sophisticated as he leans on the bar with one hand in his pocket and the other wrapped around a crystal tumbler.

He doesn't see us at first, or if he does, he doesn't stop his conversation. I don't know who the man he's talking to is, but clearly he takes priority. My mother pushes on my back, navigating me toward Davis.

I think if we were a real couple he'd stop talking as soon as I entered the room. His eyes would lock onto me, scanning my body like it was the most beautiful piece of art he'd ever seen. I think if this were real, he'd walk to me slowly, matching my steps. He'd wrap an arm around my waist and drag my body toward him. All the while, his eyes would be locked on me, admiring me. Then he'd kiss me, his lips pressing against mine gently, waiting for the invitation to deepen the kiss, which I would give him. Because if this were real, I'd be looking at him the same way. Admiring his good looks, the way his lips tick up into the sexiest smile.

But this isn't real.

Instead, my fiancé snaps his fingers at me, gesturing for me to come closer. When I do, his eyes rake over my body, but not in an appreciative way. I feel like I'm being judged, like I might receive a report card at the end of this endeavor.

"You look nice," he tells me when his eyes finally stop their assessment. He wraps an arm around my waist, bringing me close to him while he snaps at the bartender. "Water with lemon for her." When the woman gets close enough, he leans onto the counter to face her. "And no alcohol, understood?" She nods her head, avoiding my gaze at all costs while she fetches my water.

My leash feels too tight. Suffocatingly tight.

Davis hands me the glass of water and brings his own glass of dark liquid to his lips. My throat itches for the burn that I know accompanies whatever alcohol is in that cup. I've grown to love the sting of it, letting it burn a trail to my stomach. The waiting for the haze to kick in. My mouth waters at the thought of my mind being numbed, at the possibility of the endless stream of narrative that flows through my head finally being silenced.

Davis goes back to his conversation only after introducing me to the man, someone in Politics, local I think, but my brain doesn't comprehend the name or the title. It's already begun filtering out useless information.

My thoughts have started to spiral, landing on my

sister again.

I can picture Lily in a white dress so vividly. She would have been a beautiful bride. My sister was stunning in a sort of an effortless way. And she was fun. God, she would probably be prancing through this party, stopping at every group of people, greeting them with big hugs and warm smiles. She wasn't fake in the way that my mother is. She didn't come off as superficial. Lily was genuine, the type of girl people wanted to be around.

Her social abilities always amazed me. Even when we were kids, she was always making friends, while I was so stuck in my social anxiety it took effort for me to even talk to someone. I didn't become comfortable in my skin until I reached high school. And then, before I even got to walk across the stage, my sister was gone.

I let my eyes flicker to Davis. The man is too arrogant to even notice me, and if he did, he would probably think I was admiring his looks, not silently blaming him for Lily's suicide.

His arm is still wrapped around my waist while he talks. We look every bit the perfect couple. Our relationship is equivalent to a pretty family portrait hung over the mantle. We're dressed nicely, our lips turned up into smiles. But beneath that one moment, that quick glimpse, we're cracking. Paint chips off the canvas. Underneath my perfectly painted face is a girl who's crumbling at the seams. And Davis, with his expensive clothes and fancy title, isn't doing much better. A sane man wouldn't be okay with someone dying, so they didn't have to marry him.

He should be the broken one.

He should be the one crying himself to sleep at night, but instead it's me.

I become Davis's anchor for the night, attached to his every move. He leads me around the restaurant with a hand pressed to my back. I feel like a pretty doll, made up just for him to show off. He introduces me to people whose names escape my brain almost immediately. They look at us with tilted heads and cute smiles, like we're such a pretty couple.

I have to wrack my brain for a way out of his grip. I need to get away, breathe in some fresh air that isn't tainted by his cologne and his grip on me. "I have to go to the bathroom," I whisper to him.

Davis' eyes dart to me and the conversation he was having pauses. I blink rapidly, I wasn't paying attention to anything outside the thoughts in my head to know what I just interrupted.

"I'll be right back," I add before tugging out of his grip and making a quick exit. I head for the balcony, slipping out the glass doors and letting the cool December air hit my face. I find myself heading for the railing, wrapping my fingers around the iron and leaning on it for support. My breath comes out in quick pants, my head spiraling with waves of thoughts.

I can't remember if I was always like this, or if my anxiety sprung to life after Lily's death. Either way, the feeling chokes me. I can't suck in enough air, can't process the oxygen.

"Hey." A hand clasps onto my shoulder and I shudder with the breath that flows to me, as if that connection to the real world finally lets me breathe again. "Lana, are you okay?"

I spin around, leaning against the iron railing so I can face my cousin. John Vitale is a whole five years older than me. When we were kids, he ran around with Lily and Sam, playing games in the green grass behind Grandfather's mansion. Sam walks up behind him and for a brief moment I see the kids I grew up with and not the men who stand in front of me.

At what point did we stop being kids? When did we shed our innocence, letting it drip away from us like melting popsicles on the Fourth of July? I can still see their baby faces in the back of my mind, but the men here with me have sharp jaw lines and dark eyes.

"Are you okay?" John asks, and it's only then that I remember he had asked me a question.

"Yes," I say. "No," I add quickly. "I don't know."

John chuckles, and Sam comes closer. "Lana," Sam breathes, "I need you to stay strong, okay? I'm... I'm working on something, but I need you to stay strong. Okay?"

I don't recognize the strangled laugh that leaves my lips. "Easy for you to say," I mutter harshly. "You're not the one in the white dress."

"Fair enough," he says. "But I can't help you if you fling yourself over this balcony, do you understand?" His hands find my shoulders, squeezing into bare skin there.

His words slice through me like a knife. I don't know if he's making a jab at my sister or if he can see through me. If he can read the thoughts that spiral through my head and knows that jumping is an option. An option that's in bright flashing letters.

"Lana," he says again. "Can you do this for me? Can you be strong?"

I feel like a child again. Can I be strong? Can I be brave?

Everything in me screams no. But I nod my head at Sam and whisper a faint yes.

I can *try* to be strong.

"But hurry," I whisper.

CHAPTER FIFTEEN

Naz

SAM CALLS RIGHT BEFORE CHRISTMAS, giving me a location to meet and nothing more. I'm itching to get back to work. The money I squirreled away has started to dwindle, and it's more than just me that depends on it.

I meet Sam in a rough area of the warehouse district. He parks his shiny Audi next to my Jeep and steps out of the car, lifting a pair of aviators from his eyes. Sam is the kind of made man who always looks like he's about to make a business deal.

Clean cut in a pair of black slacks with a button-down shirt tucked in. His suit jacket is missing, probably because even in December, Louisiana is hot. The temperature fluctuates between chilly and scorching this time of year. Today falls in the scorching category.

Sam gives me an easy smile as he swings the Audi's door shut and rounds the front of the car. "Ready for your first day?" he asks.

I have no idea what Sam does or if it's even different from the jobs I did for Marcus. How stupid is that? To accept a job when you don't even know what it entails? All I know is that if Sam is true to his word and gets me my button, I won't have to worry about assholes like Marcus and Damien ever again.

I have to keep my eye on the prize, not let anything step in the way.

Again.

Stay alive. Make money. Get made.

Those are the priorities. Those are the pillars that I cling on to. That's all that matters.

Sam weaves us into the warehouse. Lifting the heavy gate and closing it once we both walk through. "This" — he gestures to the large industrial space filled with cars, or pieces of cars rather — "is the chop shop."

He smiles widely as he looks to me. "Do you like cars, Naz?"

"Yeah," I tell him, running a hand through my hair. I've loved cars since I was kid. I'm pretty sure the first job I told my mom I wanted was to be a race-car driver. The sleek paint, the engines, the speed, I love all of it. In another life I might have been a mechanic. But in this life, I needed more money than that would have offered. "Yeah, I like cars."

"Good," he says, clapping me on the shoulder. "This will be yours then."

His words don't make sense at first. I don't comprehend what he means by saying *this will be mine.*

"You'll run this crew." He waves his hand to the warehouse again. My eyes roam the open space. There are men working on the cars, removing tires and engine blocks. I know what they're doing, pulling the pieces from the car, selling everything they can individually and raking in profits. The cars are probably stolen. From the looks of it, they're all high end. A Jaguar sits in front and center, and there's a BMW behind it. There are about five men working in the warehouse. Each in casual clothing, their hands wrapped in mechanic gloves and their jeans covered in grease.

"I don't understand," I tell Sam.

"You'll run this crew," he repeats. "I'll teach you everything you need to know. This will bring in more money than what you were making from Marcus. The boys will jack the cars and sell the parts, you just need to keep them on schedule. You pay them a cut of what they bring back, and then you'll get a chunk, but you'll need to kick up a percentage to me. A high percentage, Naz." He eyes me as he says the last part.

I know how the rules work in *La famiglia*, you don't make nearly as much as the boss. That's the way it's always been. The lower rungs of the ladder do all the work, kick the dollars back up to the bosses' pocket.

But what Sam is offering takes me up more than a level on the ladder. He's offering me a whole crew. I'll be taking a cut of what all these guys make. Right now, I get a portion of what I sell and then Marcus takes the rest, presumably kicking some up to Damien. But what Sam is proposing puts me at the same level of Marcus.

I scrub a hand over my face. I was in before Sam showed me this place. The promise of protection was more than enough to hook me in. All of this is just a bonus.

A really fucking good bonus.

"Of course," I tell him. He can have seventy percent for all I care. The money I bring in here is still going to be far more than what I make now.

"Why?" I ask, the word popping from my lips before I can think better of it.

Sam shrugs, his eyes scanning over the men in the

warehouse before he answers me. "Do you like her? Lana, I mean. Do you like her or was she just an easy fuck for you?" His eyes shift back to me for a moment after he asks the question.

It's not a simple one for me to answer.

Do I like her? Yeah, but I don't know her really. At least not as much as I'd like to. It's hard to admit to someone's family that you want them when you've only met them twice. I feel like I should know more about her before I make that statement.

When's her birthday? Early riser or night owl? What's her favorite color and food and thing to do? What makes her laugh? And what brings tears to her eyes?

I need to know every little detail.

All I know right now is there's a sadness that washes over her. She carries it like a weight on her shoulders, letting it suffocate her and drag her down. She lets it go only when she's bare before me. She has to let the control go, become vulnerable on her knees in front of me. Only then does that heaviness float away from her.

I know her eyes are intoxicating. The hazel color shifts between a green hue and brown one. I could stare at them for hours, losing myself in their grasp. I know she pants when she's going to come, and she loves when I'm rough with her. Those eyes sparkle when I slap her ass or slam into her.

She wasn't a quick fuck or an easy lay. Not at all. Having Lana Romano in my bed is pure ecstasy. She tastes better than any drug I've ever had.

"Nah." I shake my head. "I mean, she wasn't an easy fuck," I tell him. "I like her."

Sam nods his head. "It won't be easy. Getting made. You'll have to work your ass off. Can you do that?"

"Yeah," I tell him. There's no way I'd say no now.

"Good," he says. "Stay loyal to me and only me, and when we open the books, I'll make sure you get a button. Okay?"

He turns to me with a look that says *capisce?* My loyalty to Sam has already been solidified. It happened the day he cut the ropes from my limbs, freeing me from my almost death. "Understood," I tell him.

"Here," he says next, tugging a white slip of paper from his pocket and handing it to me. It's a torn sheet of notebook paper with ten digits scribbled across it in thick black ink. "Lana's number," he adds. "I just had Madi drop off a burner phone. You and I are the only ones with the number."

I stare at the thick lines of the numbers. Guys like

Sam don't do anything that doesn't benefit them. So why would he give me his cousin's number? How does this benefit him? "Why?" I ask.

He shrugs, nonchalant, as if this conversation isn't life changing for him. Probably because it's not, not like it is for me anyway.

"She needs a reason to live," he says. "I think you may be that reason."

I stare at the numbers forever. They burned a hole in my pocket the entire drive back to my apartment. It was like they had a life of their own. I couldn't practically feel them vibrating.

I've been staring at them for hours. The second I got home, I plucked the paper from my pocket, pressing it out on the kitchen counter.

Should I call her?

What would I even say?

Hey, it's me? That guy you slept with who almost died because of it?

Maybe a joke. *Hey, your pussy is killer. Almost literally.*

No. That's fucking stupid. I run my hands through my hair and heave a sigh. I'm being ridiculous, acting like a child over calling a girl. I've seen her fucking naked, it shouldn't be that hard to call her.

I pull my cell phone from my pocket, jabbing at each of the numbers with my finger. The ringing feels like it takes forever, an endless stream of buzzing.

When it finally stops and her silky voice floats through the device, I'm paralyzed. I can't come up with the words to speak back to her simple *hello*.

"Hi," I finally whisper, the word coming out breathy and rough.

"Hi," she responds. "How did you—Sam?"

"Yeah, Sam gave me the number," I tell her. She sounds surprised, but the good kind of surprised. Like getting flowers for no occasion, not the unwanted but I'll-fake-it kind reserved for surprise parties and unplanned pregnancies.

I don't know what to talk about with her. I have no right to want to hear her voice. No right to take pleasure in her happiness and wallow in her grief.

She's not mine and I'm not hers.

"Are you okay?" I ask. It's the first thing I can think of, and something I need to know. The last time she was here, she was drunk. She was hovering over the edge, seconds from jumping. She needed me to numb her pain, make her feel anything else, and I happily obliged. Because I wanted the distraction too.

Is that all we are? Each other's distraction?

"Yeah," she breathes, and I can hear the crack of her breath as it hits the receiver. "No," she adds. "I don't know. Not really." Her tone is unsure, her answers changing. I can feel the anxiety coming from her, the sincerity in her pain and confusion.

"Is it him?" I ask, and again I know I don't deserve an answer, don't deserve to know how he treats her or what he does to her. Because she's not mine, and I know that. I know it with every fiber of my being. I can't have the woman on the other end of this phone call.

But I want to know.

I want to know what he did to confuse her. What words he said that eat away at her brain. What he did to make her hate herself.

And then I want to fix it for her. I want to smooth over his wreckage, ease the aches that fill her body and soul. I want to whisper sweet words to erase his voice, press soft kisses along her body to cover up his touch.

I want to burn away every reminder of him until all she can feel is me.

"Yeah," she whispers. "Him, my parents, everyone."

"Can you get away?" I ask, the words escaping

my lips in a moment of weakness. My heart takes over and utters the words my brain won't let me say.

"Now?" she asks, surprise lacing her voice.

"Yeah, can you meet me?"

She's silent on the other line but I can hear her breath, an easy flow of air. "Yeah," she says and it's fucking music to my ears. "I can meet you."

Laughter looks good on her.

We're in the outskirts of the French Quarter in a shitty dive bar, far enough from *famiglia* territory, that I don't think we'll be spotted. Lana brings the plastic cup of vodka to her lips, taking a hearty sip of the clear liquid and scowling as it burns its way down her throat. "Ugh," she groans, but then smiles softly when she turns to look at me, and it's mesmerizing. Lana has this kind of pull that I can't explain. It grasps me when she's sad, tugging me toward her. But damn, when she smiles, my heart throbs, aching inside my chest cavity. If I was attracted to a sad Lana, happy Lana only increases that attraction.

I chuckle, taking a gulp from my own cup of amber liquid. "Are you even old enough to drink?"

A smile lifts the corners of her lips, she looks best

like that, happy, not weighted down with obligations. "Nope," she says with a pop. "Not for a few months."

Age doesn't matter much in a place like this, but my gut still clenches with her admission. There are so many things wrong about sitting at this bar next to her, the first being that she's engaged.

I glance down to the rock that sits on her finger. It's a large diamond, way more than I could ever afford to buy her. She catches my gaze and covers the ring with her other hand, plucking it from her finger and slipping it into her purse.

"Sorry—"

"No," she cuts me off, "I should have taken it off at home, but my mom notices everything." She shrugs and brings the cup of alcohol back up to her lips.

I want to toss that ring in the Mississippi River.

But I have no claim to the woman next to me, the ring only serves as a reminder of that.

If Damien saw me here sitting inches away from her, he would cut my balls off.

They ache just thinking about it, but then I glance over and see her swaying with the music, full pink lips mouthing the lyrics, and I can't bring myself to leave her.

I run a hand over the stubble that covers my face. I've been waiting for an in, a place in this family.

171

Something she was just simply born into. We're different, the two of us. A stranger would just see two, twenty-something's at the bar, but the power dynamic is off. She's practically royalty, a mob princess. And I'm just a solider, a drug runner, *nothing*.

The past year I've spent running around, giving into Marcus' every whim in order for a chance to earn my button. I can't help thinking that Sam could just be stringing me along. He practically pushed me at her tonight. What if someone finds us here? It's not her who will pay for it.

But then I remember her face as she tipped back the bottle of jack and asked me to make her forget for a minute. Maybe she does pay, her payment is simply different.

There are rules that go along with this secret society. Loyalty is above all of them. We're loyal to each other, to *La famiglia,* and to our boss above all else.

The thing in New Orleans is that the Costello family is *La famiglia.* Don Carmine brought this thing of ours over from Sicily, stopping in New York for only a brief moment before heading south to Louisiana. He built this family and this city from the ground up. Before his death he named Junior as his successor, something Lana's father didn't take very well.

But I assume Damien has been planning his coup

since before Junior was named the successor. He tried to marry off Lily to Davis years ago. The only reason the deal was delayed was because she jumped off the balcony. If Lily was alive, I guarantee Davis would be five steps ahead in whatever power play he has going.

Junior and Sam must know though, they must suspect. I have the urge to ask him, see what he's planning, but that's above my pay grade and Sam has already been generous with me.

Everyone in this city respected Don Carmine, and since he named Junior his successor, they should respect him. At least, hypothetically.

My stomach clenches thinking about Damien winning the war that's brewing. What happens to Lana if Sam doesn't have a plan or if Junior can't help her? She just gets married to Davis and that's it?

"Is Naz short for something?" she asks, her eyes traveling back up to meet mine as she breaks me out of the thoughts that were running through my head.

"Ignazio."

She hums a pleasant sound, of interest I think. "Fiery," she says with a smile. This time the smile is brighter, her full lips open and her white teeth are on display for me.

Fiery.

Is that a flirt, a compliment? I'm not sure. She must sense my confusion, see the look on my face.

"*Ignis*," she says. "It's Latin for fire. Ignazio, Ignis. You're named after fire. I wonder why. Did your mom ever mention?" she says everything in a rush of words spewing from her lips. She's unfazed by the verbal vomit that just left her, bringing the plastic cup back to her lips, grimacing as she takes another swig.

"Fire," I repeat, stunned and amazed.

She looks back to be, that grin still plastered to her face. "Sorry." She laughs. "I have a thing for names. I was bored a lot as a kid."

"Why?" is all I can manage to say.

She chuckles to herself and looks at me over the rim of the plastic. "I was homeschooled for a while. Parents are crazy, remember?"

"They taught you?" I'm surprised. Damien Romano doesn't seem like one to take much interest in his daughters, if only because they're not boys. And her mother doesn't seem like the type of woman who wanted to spend much time with her kids. Every time I've seen Carlotta, she looked cold, unfeeling.

The night her older daughter leapt from a balcony is seared into my mind.

I redirect my attention back to Lana. She shakes her head to answer my question. "No, we had a teacher that came to the house."

"Wow," I say, silently adding *that is some rich person shit.* Only the extravagantly wealthy have private teachers. A step above the eliteness of the private schools. I try not to scoff. It's not her fault she was born with something that most people will never have.

"So you spent your free time learning...Latin?"

She laughs, a light breathy sound. "No. Origins. I like knowing where things come from."

"Okay." I chuckle. "What does Lana mean?"

"Slavic," she recites. "Meaning light."

"So light and fire. Seems like we could burn this place down."

CHAPTER SIXTEEN

Lana

WHEN WE STEP OUT OF the tiny dive bar, I'm buzzed.

The high of the alcohol makes me sway as I step down from the entrance and smile, laughing at myself for the show of my drunkenness. Naz chuckles too, he leans his back against the brick wall outside the bar and pulls a pack of cigarettes from his back pocket.

The act is disgusting, but there's something attractive about Naz as he lights one of the cigarettes. A small chunk of black hair strays from his mane, falling onto his face as he blows out the smoke. I feel like a high school stoner, high on the sight of him.

Maybe I'm just addicted to the only bit of happiness I've had in what feels like forever. My days have been repetitive, the only thing to shake them up is Davis' abuse.

Being with Naz is the only time I've smiled since my grandfather died.

He's the only bit of light I have. But our moments are stolen. Pockets of time we're not allowed to have. It feels forbidden, that if anyone caught us, we'd be dragged apart kicking and screaming.

And we know that, because we've been here before, driven away from each other in separate cars. Worry gnawed at me the entire time, if he would have been killed because of me, I would have never been able to live with myself.

Who am I to have such power over someone's life? That my actions could lead to life or death consequences. It grates at me, I don't want him to be punished because of me. It's not his fault that I was born to a family that doesn't value women's rights. That sees me as a currency rather than a human being.

Why should he die for that?

"You're stuck up here," Naz says, tapping his finger against the side of his skull. He takes another drag of the cigarette and I watch how his lips meet the filter, somehow feeling jealous of the cancer stick.

He's right. I am stuck in my head. Flying through thoughts of his lips on my skin and knowing how dangerous this game we're playing is.

There's a feeling buzzing through my body. I'm not sure if it's the alcohol or the high of doing something forbidden. But there's only one word I can think of to describe it: *reckless.*

"I don't know what I'm doing," I admit.

Naz smiles at my words, a kind of lopsided smirk that makes my stomach somersault. "I don't have a fucking clue, babe," he says, the words leaving his lips with a throaty laugh. "You're like fucking poison, but for some reason I want to taste every drop." He drops the cigarette, snubbing it out with the toe of his boot.

His eyes linger on the pavement before rising to meet mine. The look he gives me is different than before, he drags his bottom lip between his teeth and my thighs clench. My body is developing an automatic response to the hunger in his gaze.

"Naz," I whisper, but it doesn't come out sounding like a warning. It's breathy and high pitched.

"Lana," he says, his voice mocking me. "Just say the word." His tone is daring, but I think we both want to repeat our mistakes.

Leaning in, he presses his lips against mine. It feels like jumping off a cliff. As soon as our mouths meet I feel the chords snap. I'm no longer attached to my parents. No longer engaged. The weight of my body drifts away and I forget all of it.

His hands find my arms and his fingers squeeze into my flesh. The bite brings me to life, hooks me into the moment. I can't get into his Jeep fast enough. My hands refuse to leave him, my fingers ache to feel him, to touch every inch of his body.

I'm addicted to the moment as my heart pounds in my chest and I can't get his jeans down fast enough. His tongue darts across his lips and I think he feels this too. He leans into me, slamming the back door of the Jeep closed behind him. I can feel the throb in his chest, his heart beating so loudly, matching the frantic rhythm of my own.

My skin burns underneath the heat of his touch. He slides the skirt of my dress up, baring my panties. His lips form a sensual smirk as his fingers race along the edge of the fabric feeling the wetness already gathered there. "How fucking needy are you for me, babe?"

My breath hitches at his question and he chuckles lowly as he swipes a finger beneath the fabric. He tugs the material to the side and slips in a finger.

I moan immediately from the sensation.

"I almost died because of you," he whispers, and I think he should be angrier. Or maybe sound more

scared. But he states it like a fact. Just a piece of information we both know.

"Maybe they'll bury me next to you," I retort,
wrapping my fingers around his wrist and pushing
him down further. I need his touch, need him to take
care of me in the way only he can.

His eyes flicker with amusement and the sight
makes me smile. I want to see that look again. Want
to be the one that makes his eyes gleam. I can picture
waking up to that smile, letting it be the first thing I
see every day.

"Oh, baby." He laughs. "They'll burn us."

I push all the thoughts from my head. I don't remind myself that we're both playing with a loaded
gun. That this could all end in a moment, a single
shot and it's over.

Life.

Death.

Everything just hangs in the balance.

Instead, I focus my attention on the man in front
of me. Let my fingers run over his smooth skin. I trail
my hands over his abs, bringing them low enough to
undo the belt around his waist.

"Are you sure this is a good idea?" It's the only
glimpse of hesitation he's given me.

"I'm sure," I tell him. I don't know if it's a truth or

a lie. But I want this, and I'm tired of sacrificing these moments of happiness. I'm exhausted from morphing myself into a different person. The acting skills have taken their toll, and I no longer like that version of myself.

I don't want to be the version of Lana that lets people push her around.

I like this version. This girl who sees what she wants and takes it.

Around Naz, I feel like myself.

He helps me free himself from his jeans and my hand finds his cock, wrapping around the thick surface. He groans as soon as my fingers touch him. I tug my bottom lip between my teeth as he takes his dick from me, pumping it quickly before he lines himself up with my entrance.

I suck in a sharp breath as he thrusts forward. He stretches me out in the best way, soothing the ache inside me.

"More," I moan. He complies by thrusting back into me. One arm wraps around the curve of my waist and the other reaches forward, taking my face in his palm. He traces his thumb over the surface of my lip, and I suck the digit into my mouth, savoring the salty taste of his skin on my tongue.

"Fuck," he moans.

My eyes roll into the back of my head as I meet him thrust for thrust. My back hits the side of the door and my head touches the glass of the window. He has one hand pressed to the doorframe and the other finds my tit. He squeezes it before bringing my nipple between his fingers.

My hands find his shoulder, my fingernails digging into his flesh.

I'm simultaneously overwhelmed and can't get enough.

My body buzzes, every nerve ending on fire and when I finally fall over the edge of my orgasm I'm screaming his name. We're both flushed and breathless when he finally pulls out, painting my skin with his cum.

We're playing with fire.

And eventually, everything is going to burn.

Naz makes me a grilled cheese sandwich. The sight of him standing at the stove in nothing but a pair of shorts has heat burning between my thighs again.

It's not an exceptional sandwich by any means. Two slices of Kraft singles between white bread. He sets the golden sandwich on the counter with a triumphant flourish.

He smiles at me, his eyes crinkling at the corners. The whole thing is so mundane. So average.

I can imagine myself coming home from school, tossing my bag by the door, and meeting him at this counter. He would press a kiss to my temple and ask me how my day was. Butterflies swarm in my stomach at the thought.

What would it be like to be his?

Naz brings the crispy sandwich to his lips, biting through the crust and moaning slightly. We were both starving when he drove us back to his apartment, another mistake added to our long list.

I've never had a man cook for me. I don't think my father has ever even set foot in the kitchen. And my mother isn't much of a housewife either, we've always had staff to cook for us. I cringe at the thought, at how naive and spoiled that sounds.

Here, in this apartment with Naz, I've finally realized how incredibly sheltered I've been. How hidden from the rest of the world I must have been to think that I was normal.

Now that I've burst through the bubble my family created, I can't go back. I can't unlearn what I now know.

I feel like I'm running. Like my feet are pounding against the pavement, taking me somewhere else. Somewhere better.

And I can't go back to how things were, because I'm not that girl anymore and I won't shove myself back into a box that doesn't fit me.

Naz watches me as he eats, almost as if he can see the thoughts that spiral through my head.

"Whatever you're thinking, babe," he says, "it's not good."

"Probably not," I tell him, lifting the grilled cheese and taking my first bite. I can't help the moan that leaves my lips at the simple sandwich. The buttery crust, the melted cheese, there's no reason for this sandwich to taste so damn good. I can't tell if it's because he made it or if I've been so busy living this extravagant life that I've never been able to step back and be *simple*.

Our chefs didn't cook like this. Lily and I were eating gourmet meals from the second we learned how to hold a fork and spoon.

Naz chuckled beside me. "If you tell me you've never had a grilled cheese, I will faint."

"Not like this," I tell him, taking another bite.

"Rich people," he says with a throaty laugh. "You over complicate everything."

He's not wrong. I shrug in response and take another bite.

This.

This simplicity, the effortless banter, I think this is what life is supposed to be.

There's a feeling, like a piece of string is tugging me toward Naz, connecting the two of us with a single line. I can't help the way the corners of my lips tug up into a smile at everything he says. His eyes sparkle and I become lost in them.

I think this is how you're supposed to feel about someone, this happiness is how you're supposed to exist.

Why is there so much pain and suffering when we could all have *this*?

"Tell me what you're thinking," he says, his curious gaze locked on me.

"I never learned how to…*be with someone*. But this, this thing between us just *feels right*. Do you know what I mean?"

Naz's eyes glance away for only a moment as he dusts the crumbs from his hands. "I do," he whispers, and for the first time tonight I can sense the fear that lingers in his words.

I'm waiting for the *but*, waiting for all the reasons why we shouldn't be here to come rushing back.

But they don't.

"I don't want to ruin this moment," I whisper.

"Me neither." His hand reaches forward, locking his fingers around mine.

"My dad is having an affair," I blurt out, the fact leaving my lips like a dirty secret. Which it's not.

It's not uncommon for men in our family to have *goomahs*, I just wish I didn't know about it.

"And I don't understand," I continue saying, "because he and Ma are like a power couple. They love each other more than me, I think."

"It's not about that." Naz says, "There's a difference between sex and love, they don't always go together."

"You don't think sex equals love?" The question comes out harsher than I meant for it, but Naz doesn't look offended.

He smiles slightly as he answers me. "Nah, you're missing what I'm saying. Sex doesn't always have a connection, sometimes it's just for simple pleasure. But if you get both, the sex and the connection, well that's just...amazing." His eyes lift to meet mine as he says the last word and my heart pounds in the walls of my chest.

"And what do we have?" I lick my lips, waiting for his answer to my hushed question.

A lopsided smirk rises on Naz's face. "What do

you think?"

I know without a doubt that what we have isn't just sex.

But I'm terrified that I'm wrong. The fear of blowing up my entire world and his over something that was just a quick mistake clouds my judgement.

Because even though I can feel our connection in my soul, I'm terrified of what that means.

"I don't know how to do this," I whisper.

"No one does." He squeezes my hand, the gesture reassuring me and anchoring me back to this moment. "We all just pretend, and we fuck up a lot. You're not perfect, Lana, but here's a secret: no one is."

My heart is pounding, every nerve ending burning as I lean forward and press my lips to his.

I don't know what tomorrow holds. I don't even know where we'll end up in a week. And maybe it will be locked in a tomb at the Lafayette Cemetery.

But I think, for this moment, it'll be worth it.

CHAPTER SEVENTEEN

Lana

I'M COATED WITH WARMTH. BETWEEN Naz's arm wrapped around me and the blanket covering my body I feel hot, but I don't want to move, don't want to risk this moment coming to an end.

This is just sex. I have to remind myself of the fact every few seconds or I'll forget. I'll get too comfortable in this moment and I won't be able to leave. And eventually I need to leave.

I didn't mean for this to happen, for these feelings to catch up to me.

But being with Naz shifts my perspective. He makes me forget about the outside world and all of rounds me and forgetting that there's a life outside of his apartment.

Blue light radiates from the TV and Naz strokes my hair with a soft touch. I wonder what he's thinking. Does his mind shift to the time? Counting down the seconds until this all dissipates?

"You're doing it again." His voice is so soft when he says the words, his eyes still on the TV, his fingers still threaded through my hair.

"What are you talking about?" I ask.

A finger taps my head, and he draws a little circle in the spot. "You're overthinking. I can practically feel it."

He looks down at me, brushing his knuckles against my cheek.

"I...I can't stop it," I admit.

He leans forward, placing a gentle kiss to my forehead. I have to remind myself again, *this isn't love.* This isn't a relationship. There is no happily ever after or riding off into the sunset. At some point I have to walk out of here, back into the grasp of my monster.

This is just a slight reprieve.

"You're trying to talk yourself into something," he says. "I can see the gears turning, your mind is spinning, huh?"

I'm amazed that he can put the feelings in my

head into words. How can he see that just from sitting here? How can he possibly tell that my mind is racing, speeding through possibilities and scenarios when I just want to breathe?

"I do the same thing," he says, as if reading the question from my face.

"How do you stop it?"

He shrugs his shoulders. "Sometimes it's harder than others, sometimes I just sink into the feeling. But other times I just need a distraction, something to take over my focus."

A distraction, I think, would be perfect. One more time? That's okay, right? I'm already here, already in his arms. Just one more time.

"Can you distract me then?"

A smile tugs at his lips, he looks heavenly like that, I think. Even with the dark ink that marks his skin, the intricate patterns that climb his arms and reach for his neck, there's something peaceful about Naz.

"Give me one sec." He presses another kiss to my forehead, and lifts my head so he can get up from the couch. He's digging through his nightstand for a moment before he comes back.

"Come on, angel." He wiggles his fingers at me, gesturing for me to get up. Grabbing a sweatshirt from his dresser, he tosses the article of clothing at me along with a pair of basketball shorts. I'm drowning in his clothes, but it's better than getting dressed in mine again.

Naz wears a pair of low hanging sweatpants and a white t-shirt that I can see his tattoos through. "Come on," he says again, taking my hand and dragging me toward the door. He pulls me over to the elevator, taking us to the top floor where the doors open to the rooftop of his building.

"Wow," I whisper. From his roof, you can see the whole neighborhood. Naz is a few blocks from the French Quarter, and I can see the lights from the bars from here, hear the faint sound of music. "This is beautiful."

"I know." He wraps his arms around my waist and presses his body against my back. "I love this view."

I could stand like this forever, with his arms wrapped around me, staring at the city I love.

"Here." Naz removes one hand, reaching into his pocket and pulling out a joint and a lighter. "Have you smoked before?"

My mouth waters at the sight, but I shake my head. I've never smoked, I was far too good to go down that road. But now? The idea of blurring my mind is intoxicating. Just something to loosen me a bit, the pot lets the thoughts and obligations weighing on me feel a little lighter.

I spin to face him, and he takes back his other hand, using it to hold the joint while he lights it with the other. I watch him intently as he brings the pot to his lips, inhaling the smoke before blowing out a white cloud.

"You don't have to," he says as he extends the joint to me.

I know I don't have to, but I want to. What a difference between those two words. Have versus want. I *have* to do a lot of things, like marry a man who makes me sick to my stomach. But I *want* to be here, on this rooftop, smoking with Naz.

I bring the joint to my lips, pulling just a bit of smoke before I cough it out. I don't smoke nearly as smooth as he does, and he chuckles as he takes the joint back from me to take another hit.

Under the moonlight, his dark eyes sparkle as they watch me. After another hit, my body is lighter and the faint sound of the music feels intoxicating. I want to dance, and I feel my body swaying to the rhythm. Naz's arms find my waist and he sways with me.

Warmth. I feel it again, traveling up my spine and

coating me in a sweet sensation. Everything feels right with him. I smile more than I ever have, my heart beats with excitement. I can't help the laughter that escapes my lips as he dips me low, then pulls me back up and presses his lips to mine.

My heart flutters, my nerve endings light up.

His fingers travel under the loose sweatshirt, roaming on my skin until they find my tits. At the same time I run my hands over his tattooed forearms, traveling lower to the waistband of his sweats and dipping beneath the band.

"What if someone comes up here?" I ask through breathy pants.

"What if?" he repeats, a devilish smirk on his lips.

The statement excites me. What if we get caught? It won't really matter, will it?

Because at the end of the day, we can't be together.

At some point, this will all come crashing down to a fiery ending.

But right now, we're here.

Our bodies are intertwined, our hearts racing in tandem. So what if this won't last, if it all has to come to an end. Right now, I want this. So I drop down to my knees, letting them hit the rough cement that covers the rooftop. I pull his cock free from the sweatpants, it's hard and thick waiting for me.

A moan leaves his lips as soon as my tongue touches the head of his cock. I lick up his length, tasting every inch of his shaft.

"Fuck," he moans, and I take pride in the sounds I elicit from him. "Come here," he growls, pulling me from his cock with a pop and lifting me up. He takes me over to the edge, placing my hands against the concrete barrier. From here, I can see the lights of the city.

"Can you keep quiet while I fuck you?" he whispers.

I flip my hair over my shoulder so I can look back at him. He looks feral with his need, gripping his cock in one hand while the other rubs over my ass. "Maybe." I smirk.

He chuckles as he tugs his shorts down my legs, exposing my bare sex. His hand comes between my legs, swiping through my slit to find me dripping. "Oh, angel." He smiles. "I love finding you wet for me." He flicks his finger over my clit, making my legs shake with need before he finally lines himself up with my sex.

When he pushes into me, I feel full and my mind feels light. The pot has loosened me up, made my mind free.

Every thrust feels like heaven, and it doesn't take long before I'm meeting his strokes, my body on edge. He wraps an arm around my body, bringing his hand to my cunt and finding my clit. His finger swirls around the bundle of nerves with precision.

I can feel my orgasm building, the heat pooling in my low stomach as he fucks me.

It takes everything in me not to scream his name as I fall over the edge. My hand covers my mouth and tears leak from my eyes as I fall. It feels like flying, the mixture of the pot and the orgasm takes me to a new level.

Naz pulls his cock from me, stroking himself and painting my back with his cum.

"Fuck, angel," he moans, leaning over to breathe into my ear. "I don't think I'll ever get enough of you."

CHAPTER EIGHTEEN

Lana

THE WHITE DRESS FEELS SUFFOCATING. The corset top digs into my skin, constricting my lungs. "I don't like it," I tell my mother, tugging at the top of the bodice.

"Hush." She slaps my fingers away. "I like this one. What you think, Rina?"

Aunt Caterina assesses the gown, inspecting the stitching as if she knows what she's looking for. I meet Madi's gaze, and she rolls her eyes at her mother. I'm thankful to have one person in my corner even if neither of our opinions matter.

"Ma," I try again, but she darts her eyes to me, giving me a look that makes my mouth snap shut. She doesn't want to hear my opinion, clearly.

"It's good," Aunt Caterina says, clapping her

hands together. "I think this is the one."

My stomach sinks, a sickness rolling through it. I can't imagine what my wedding day will look like. Can't even fathom walking down the aisle in this dress.

The wedding, planned by a professional who only listens to my mother's opinions, is an extravagant affair.

It feels like most of New Orleans will be there, between my parents' guest list and Davis'. The wedding bears no resemblance to me. If my name wasn't on the invitation, I don't think anyone would even know it was mine.

Isn't this supposed to be a day girls dream about?

My only dreams are about how to get out of this.

I think about begging, right here, in this too tight dress. Sinking to the ground like a petulant child. But she won't care.

So instead, I stay silent.

When I come out of the dressing room in my jeans and t-shirt, it's just Madi left. My mom and Caterina went to the front of the bridal shop to pay for the grand dress.

Madi looks at me with a sympathetic look. "Ma told me I'd have to dye my hair for your wedding."

The comment surprised me and I can't help but

laugh. "What did you say?"

"Fuck that." Madi giggles and steps closer to me. She wraps her arms around me, pulling me into her chest. "I'm sorry," she whispers. She has no reason to apologize, nothing is her fault, but still the sympathy makes me feel slightly better.

I hug her back and we stay like that for a moment, both silently recognizing how fucked up our family is.

I don't hate the idea of a white dress or of marriage. I hate the situation, the man I'll be meeting at the end of the aisle. I hate that I wasn't given a choice.

I take a look at the dress hanging on the door of my fitting room. There's no one else around, we're in our private area, a special fitting for clientele of our "status."

A thought pops into my head as I stare at the white fabric that was just on my body.

I don't think too hard about it as I pull the tube of red lipstick from my purse, pushing up the red crayon from its bullet casing.

It takes two steps for me to be in front of the dress before I'm coloring it with the lipstick. I slash a bright smear of red across it, letting the color stain the white fabric.

Relief floods my body.

The action gives me a rush. It feels cathartic, and I can't stop my hand from continuing the motions, covering the white fabric with the red wax until my arms are sore.

Madi stares at me with wide eyes.

When I'm done, the lipstick used down until there's nothing left but a little nub, I'm panting.

"That was badass," Madi says, her lips still forming a wide 'O' in shock.

It won't matter, the dress is only a try-on version, the real one will still be ordered.

But the feeling, the release it gave me, was well worth it.

I stare at my work as my breathing evens out.

I'm a fighter.

I repeat the words in my mind like a mantra.

I'm not going down without a fight.

"I heard about your little *scene* while dress shopping." There's a smirk playing on Davis' face when he sits next to me. The love seat in my parents' living room suddenly feels crowded.

Instantly, my heels press against the ground, ready to push me to a standing position, my flight response kicking in.

Davis reaches across my thighs, effortlessly pushing me back down so my ass hits the cushions. "No," he growls under his breath.

Behind us somewhere, his mother is talking to mine about wedding details while our fathers' bicker over sports. Each of them acts like nothing else is going on here, like there's *nothing wrong*. While I feel like a thousand-pound weight is pressed to my chest. Maybe for his parents, this is normal. What if they don't even know what kind of terrible person they raised? They've never seen the marks his fingers can make. Never seen the tick in his jaw when he gets angry.

Later, they'll go to Davis' brothers for their second Christmas Eve celebration of the night, dragging me along. I don't get choices anymore, just orders delivered through text messages.

I suck in a breath, hoping the oxygen will settle me. I refuse to cower next to him. I don't want to be the type of woman who shrinks next to a man, so I steel my spine and try to mentally block him out.

"Lana," he coos, in the sickly-sweet voice that experience has proven means something else. This man isn't sweet, he puts on a show right before he says something menacing.

There's a quick moment where I remember the feeling of my body hitting the tiled floor when he pushed me, the trickle of blood running down my forehead. I shove the memory away, not allowing my emotions to take over.

"We don't have to talk," I say, in the harshest voice I can muster while still avoiding his eyes.

He chuckles beside me, the sound a deep rumble. "I don't think you understand how this works, doll."

It takes everything in me to stay strong, to not turn my gaze, or squirm under his scrutiny. He leans in closer to me, his breath skating over my neck. He shifts my hair out of the way with a single finger as he brings his lips to my ear.

"You do whatever the fuck I tell you. Do you understand that?"

I flinch, and immediately I scold myself for the show of weakness.

Maybe I'm not strong, maybe I'm not a warrior. It takes every ounce of energy I have to pull myself together.

"No," I mutter. "I don't." I turn my head, meeting his gaze for the first time. "I would have to respect you for that to happen."

His gaze darkens, it feels like something shifts, his patience snapping. And before I can register what's happening, his hand darts forward, closing the space between us as his fingers wrap around my throat.

He stands pulling me up with him as he rises. My fingers come to his grasp, tugging at his skin trying to pull him off me, but it doesn't stop him. His other hand comes to my neck, joining the first in squeezing the delicate flesh.

Somewhere in the background I hear a gasp and the footsteps, but they're not coming toward me. The door swings and closes, and I become suddenly aware that no one is coming to my rescue. Not even my own mother.

I guess power does that to you.

The lure of it is so delicious that you would sacrifice anything.

And for my mother, my worth equals whatever I can provide her. I'm just a bargaining chip, a game piece meant to take her further in life. And right now, I'm getting in the way of her plans.

It's becoming harder to breathe as his fingers dig into my neck. My head becomes foggy, a pain shooting through it. I'm terrified, but a sick part of me wants him to squeeze harder. Wants him to squeeze every ounce of life from me.

At least that way, I won't have to do this anymore.

"You don't get a say, Lana," he says the words

with such venom that spit flies from his lips and hits my skin.

I close my eyes, sinking into the feeling of being unable to breathe, trying not to struggle.

Just let it happen.

"That was rude, ruining that dress. Do you know whose pocket that came out of?" He brings his lips to my ear, his breath warming the skin there. "I told your parents I would cover it, said I had overstepped. And you know what they did, Lana?" I can feel his lips curl upward, his face so close to mine. "They apologized." He laughs, a low rumble. "I hit you, and they apologized. So whatever you're thinking in this silly head of yours, let it go, baby. No one gives a fuck."

But before I sink off into oblivion, he lets go.

With no support, my body crashes to the ground, my arm banging off the coffee table as I slump down. I heave a breath, my lungs tasting the oxygen as if for the first time. It takes a few panting breaths before I can finally breathe, the fog lifting from my head. I roll onto my side, my fingers grasping against the floor.

"Do as you're told, Lana," Davis growls, hovering over me. "Or you won't like the consequences."

CHAPTER NINETEEN

Naz

I'M WIPING THE GREASE FROM my hands onto a rag while admiring the new pearl white Lexus Jimmy just drove into the shop when Sam walks in. He whistles low as his eyes scan across the pricey vehicle. "Chop or overseas?" he asks, shoving his hands into the pockets of his gray dress slacks. Sam has bed head, or at least the hair of someone who runs his fingers through it nonstop, but the rest of him looks polished. He has on a pair of pressed slacks with a button-down tucked into them, foregoing the tie and jacket, probably because even in January, NOLA is hot.

'Overseas," I tell him, tossing the dirty rag onto a bench behind me. "Boss." I nod my head to him in a short greeting. It's the formalities in this organization that hold the most weight. Men with power like to be reminded that they're in charge, they like to make sure that every single soldier knows it. And if you don't, he'll make sure you do.

Jimmy, the kid who drove in the Lexus, learned that the hard way. He clutches his right hand whenever he sees Sam, as if he can protect it from the damage that's already done. The kid tried to steal a part from one of the cars he stole and Sam found out. He strolled into the shop with a drill in hand, had his men hold Jimmy down and then drilled through the nails and fingertips of two fingers. Cody, one of the other guys who works in the shop, told me the story in a hushed tone while Jimmy was out stealing a different car. In his words, "Jimmy was fucked up after that."

He moves to the back of the shop, walking toward a tool bench and pretending to grab something. From working with him the past month, I've learned his antics. He probably doesn't need a damn thing, he just doesn't like to be around Sam.

If someone drilled a hole through my fingers, I don't think I'd want to be near them either.

"That'll make a decent penny," Sam says, a smile rising on his cheeks.

He's not wrong though. One of his men will be

here within thirty minutes to pick up the Lexus, putting it in a shipping container and sticking it on a ship. The captain will take a stack of hundreds to add the container, no questions asked.

At the port in Europe, another man will grab the container, load it up and from there, I don't know the rest of the details. It's better that way, if I can't connect the entire process. If someone picks me up, the most they can get is what happens in my shop. Sam might be the only one who knows the entire process, but once the car is out of the States, even he doesn't know all of the hands it exchanges.

The money from the car gets wired to an offshore account, and from there we'll split the profit. Jimmy will get a cut for stealing the car, I get a cut for running the shop, and Sam will take the rest.

I can't complain though because the money that ends up in my hands is a lot. Far more than when I worked for Marcus. A month with Sam and I'm already set up well.

"How's the kid?" Sam asks, directing his attention from the car back to me.

For being one of the toughest criminals in New Orleans, Sam has a soft spot. I told him I was struggling to get the new PlayStation for Anthony, the only thing the kid wanted for Christmas. The new model was sold out everywhere. Next day, he had a man drop off a truckload of them. Hijacked the truck delivering the electronics and suddenly we had a hundred PlayStations ready to resell and one ready to be wrapped up for Christmas.

So despite the holes in Jimmy's finger, I wasn't afraid of Sam Costello. He valued loyalty above all else, and as long as I was loyal to him, I trusted he'd be loyal to me.

"Thrilled." I laugh. "Ma's a little pissy she can't get him away from the TV, but you should see his ranking in COD."

Sam laughs. "Good." Something flickers in his eyes for a moment, and he ticks his head to the side, gesturing for me to move away from the car and out of the earshot of the men.

I follow him without question to the corner of the shop. "What's up, boss?" Since putting me in charge of this shop, Sam had given me dozens of side projects. Selling stolen goods, fetching shipments, shadowing deals. I do each task with no complaints. Seeing each mission as a step closer to that golden button, to the possibility of not having to sleep with a gun under my mattress.

Sam drags a hand through his dark hair, messing it up further. "Have you spoken to Lana?" he asks.

Talking about his cousin is a weird topic between us. He's pushing me toward her, and I haven't quite figured out his end game. I can't believe it's because he wants her to be happy or that he thinks I love her. Men like him, like his family, don't value feelings such as *love*. And they're selfish. Everything has a dollar amount next to it, even Lana.

I have to think that he has a plan, some kind of angle he's working on. I just don't know what I have to do with it.

My phone burns in my pocket. I text the burner phone every morning and every evening. The only times we talk is when she's hidden in her room. Otherwise, she keeps the phone off, tucked away in a drawer where her family won't find it. It's weird, I think, to have a relationship based on only talking at two specific times a day.

And only through text message. I haven't heard her voice since the last time she was in my apartment, her body tucked under my sheets. But that was over a month ago. I think of the image daily though. More than just the sex, I love revisiting the face she makes as she cums around my cock. But also, the smile etched across her cheeks as she took a bite of the grilled cheese I made her.

The messages on the blue lit screen aren't enough

for me, but the other option is nothing. So I take what I can get.

I pull my cell from my pocket, opening up my chat with Lana. Last message was at 9 am, she never responded then.

"Not today," I tell him, sliding the device back into my pocket.

Sam chews on his lip for a second before regaining his composure. It's funny, he's always put together. I've never seen an ounce of fear or worry on this man except for the brief second just now.

"What's going on?" I ask. "Is she okay?"

Sam sighs heavily. "It's a little worse than I anticipated," he says, the words leaving his lips in a calm demeanor, giving me no inkling into what worse actually means.

Thoughts race through my mind. Is she dead? Hurt?

"Is she okay?" I ask again, feeling like a broken record.

"She's alive," Sam says. "And I need you to keep her that way," he adds the second part in a stern voice and grimly. No longer are we talking about the welfare of his cousin. Now he's giving me an order.

"What does that mean?" I ask, trying my best not to sound defiant. The thing about our relationship that works, is that I don't ask questions. Sam gives me a job and I complete it. But this isn't a job for me, this is a person we're talking about.

"You need to see her. Make sure no one sees you though. Ya know what I mean?" He looks at me expectantly.

He's telling me to see her discreetly. "What makes you think that I can help her?" I ask him. My patience with his game is wearing thin. I trust Sam, at least I think I do. But whatever he's playing here, it's dangerous. I already almost died from seeing Lana, and the fact that he wants me to visit her discreetly, tells me there's still a chance that will happen.

Sam's lips turn upward, just enough to give me a small reassuring smile. "She's happier after she sees you. She's stronger too. When she sees you, she handles him better, less fear, ya know."

"This will help," he says, slipping a scrap of paper into my hand. "Make it happen, Naz." He grins, spinning on his heel and leaving my shop.

Just make it happen.

Easy for him to say.

There are only two words and a single number scribbled on the piece of paper Sam gives me, *Lafayette Cemetery 1*. The place is located in The Garden District, a nice area of the city where rich people are buried.

On the street, blocking the entrance, is a black SUV. In the driver's seat, I see one of Damien's enforcers, a tough and big guy named Tony. His hand dangles out the window, a cigarette perched between his fingertips.

I'm not sure what kind of mission Sam is sending me on, but the tone in his voice no longer made me feel like there was an option. The slip of paper laying in my palm felt like an order.

Not that it mattered.

Semantics, really.

Because seeing Lana doesn't feel like an obligation. A death wish, maybe, but not an obligation. Duty isn't stopping me from seeing her, it's the enforcers that guard her from me.

I pull back onto the road, going around the block to the back of the cemetery. If I'm lucky, there will be a second entrance. I park my Jeep on the street behind the cemetery, letting it blend in with the other cars on the block.

My eyes scan the surroundings before I cross the street, looking for anyone who might notice I'm up to something. Down the street, a couple walks with their dog, their attention focused on each other. On the other side, an older man ambles down the sidewalk, his eyes downcast.

I make my way to the opposite sidewalk facing the back of the cemetery. The graveyard is surrounded by an iron fence. The rows of metal don't do much to keep people out though, the thing is barely as tall as me and it only takes moderate effort for me to climb and lift my body weight over the top. The only real deterrence is the decorative spikes that protrude from the iron every few feet, but it's easy enough to avoid them.

My feet thud against cobble stone as I land in the graveyard. The tombs stand tall in long rows, towering above the ground. I'm not sure where the Costello tombs sit in this place, but I'm sure that's where she is.

I start walking in search for her. It feels wrong being here, sneaking into such a sacred place to find a girl I'm not supposed to be with.

I turn right, into another row of tombs. Angels carved from stone hover above me as I walk, and for a second I think I can feel their judgment raining down on me. I never much believed in religion, never thought too long about God, even as my Catholic mother dragged my ass to church every Sunday.

But my roots have taken a bigger hold on me than I thought, because I can't escape the Angels or their watching eyes. Every turn takes me into another row with another concrete angel staring at me.

I'm beginning to think I've gotten lost in the maze of tombs when I see a head of blue hair walking toward me. I turn to the closest stone, pretending to admire the details carved into the stone.

"I know who you are." The blue hair girl calls over to me. She stops, a few feet away from me, and crosses her arms over her chest.

Shit.

"Listen," I tell her, "I'm just here to see my mother." I gesture to the tomb I'm standing at.

A smile rises on her features as she steps closer peering over at the tomb. "Your mother died in 1901, huh?"

Shit.

"I'm not gonna tell on you." She laughs, leaning in closer. "I'm on Lana's side," she whispers. With a pat on the back, she passes by me. "Nice to meet you, Ignazio. She's one row over." And then she's walking away, the sound of her black chucks slapping the cobblestones getting fainter as she goes.

One row over, like she said, I find Lana. Her back

is pressed against a smooth granite stone, her head leaned back and looking toward the sky. She's dressed simply, a pair of black joggers, cinched at the ankle, and a matching black sweatshirt. Her hair is twisted and piled into a messy knot on top of her head.

Her eyes are still closed as I approach.

"Not yet," she mumbles and slowly her hazel eyes open. Shock covers her features when she sees me and immediately her hands press against the ground as she pushes herself up. "What are you doing here?" she asks in a rushed whisper.

"Someone told me you'd be here." I place my hand on her hip, tugging her toward me. I want to run my hands over her body, need to feel the smooth curves of her skin. I've never missed a person the way I miss Lana. When she's not near me, I think about remembering every inch of her face, the taste of every kiss. It feels like an addiction, like I'm just biding time until my next hit.

After my bout with cocaine, I've spent so much time keeping myself from letting drugs and alcohol consume me, refusing to follow in the footsteps of my father. But no one ever warned me about this woman. No one told me to watch out for girls who pull you in with kisses sweet as candy and eyes like gold.

"Naz," she whispers, "what if —"

"Shh." I press a finger to her lip, silencing whatever objection she had. Instead, I lean in and press my mouth against her. She meets me there, letting me tug her bottom lip between my teeth. When I finally pull back, my eyes rake over her, wanting to see every inch of her.

They stop immediately though. Her neck is covered in purple bruises, the angry color fades toward the edges and wraps around the side. I can make out four distinct lines from where his fingers curved around her throat.

My chest aches and it feels like my stomach is full of rocks. I'm not sure if I want to scream or vomit at the sight. "What happened?" I ask, the question coming out in a deep growl that makes her flinch. "I'm sorry." I step back, sucking in a breath and trying to calm myself. "Please, tell me what happened."

She steps back too, wrapping her arms around her stomach in a protective gesture. "I'm okay," she whispers, the words coming out low and meek. She's lying. I can see from the way she holds herself, the way her eyes drop down to her feet, avoiding my gaze.

"Baby," I whisper, and slowly walk toward her, extending my hand to her. She lets me pull her close again, lets her body sink into mine. I wrap my arms around her, holding her tightly.

I can feel her pull in a shaky breath, and when she meets my eyes again, hers are glassy, brimming with tears.

"It was a mistake," she says. "I shouldn't have pushed him."

I grip onto her shoulder, staring into her eyes. "This is not your fault. Do you understand me? His actions are not your fault."

She swallows thickly and her eyes dart to the side. "His anger, I should have known..."

"No," I tell her. "You shouldn't tip toe around his feelings. You can control his anger, that's up to him. And no man should ever hurt you." My eyes scan over the purple covering her throat and I can feel her watching me as I lift a finger to trace over the colors.

"You are worth so much more than this. And I hope one day you see that."

The tears that had pooled in her lower lash line break free and run down her cheeks. "I'm scared," she whispers, and I pull her closer, running my hand over her back in a circular motion.

The truth that I won't say out loud is I'm scared too.

Scared that one day he'll go too far, squeeze for too long, hit too hard.

"It's gonna be okay," I tell her. But I don't know that. I have no idea if it will be okay. If Sam does have an end game, I hope to God he starts it now.

"Here." I pull back. Her eyes watch me as I unclasp the gold chain from around my neck, bringing it to her. "Turn around," I tell her, and she complies, spinning around so I can clasp the necklace on her neck.

When she turns back to me, she's holding the gold St. Jude medal between her fingertips, her eyes cast down watching the light reflect off the charm.

"Patron saint of lost causes?" she whispers.

"Yeah, my—"

"Your grandmother gave it to you." Her eyes snap up to meet mine. "I remember, but this is important to you, you can't give it to me." Her hands reach around her neck to unclasp it, but I stop her, placing my hands over hers.

"I can," I tell her. "That medal protected me when I needed it, and now it will protect you, okay? You wear that and St. Jude will watch over you."

She brings her fingers back to the charm, and for a moment, I can see the thoughts churning through her head as her thumb runs over the pendant. "Do you really believe that?"

"I'm here, aren't I?" Her eyes flicker to mine.

"What did it protect you from?"

Her question makes the scar on my thigh twitch, like the simple memory can bring the pain back to life. I rub my hand down the denim covering it, trying to soothe the ache that's building there. "My father," I tell her.

"What he'd do?" she asks, her curious gaze fixed on my face.

"When I was a kid, he was in a rough place, still might be, I'm not sure. But his mother, my grandma, wanted contact with us kids even though he was out of the picture. So my ma took me and Elly there every Sunday after church. My grandmother — she gave me this." I point to the charm now hanging from her throat. "Said she'd had it since she was a little girl. Someone had given it to her for their journey from Palermo to the States." I swallow, unsure if I should tell her the next part of the story. "Her parents... died on the ship, but she didn't. Since then, she believed the medal protected her."

Lana blinks quickly. "That's horrible," she whispers.

"The day she gave it to me, my father came over to her house. He was going through withdrawal, looking for cash to get his next fix. She hid Elly and I in the bedroom when she saw him coming because she didn't want us to see our father like that, ya know? But she didn't have her medal because she had given it to me. So, I went out to help her. My father was in the kitchen, with a knife. When I ran for her, he waved the damn thing, making a six-inch cut down my thigh." Instinctively, I touch the spot where he cut me.

"Naz," she whispers, her eyes teary again.

"Missed everything vital." I let a small smirk rise on my lips. "It might sound silly, Lana, but that medal made me go check on my grandma and we both lived."

"But he cut you," she breathes.

"But I lived."

Her glassy eyes find mine and she leans against me, letting me hold her close. "But you lived," she repeats my words, holding the medal close to her heart. "But you *lived*."

CHAPTER TWENTY

Lana

I FEEL LIKE A DOLL on Davis' arm, just an ornament on display. A pretty object to make him look good, a successful man with a pretty woman. It's a silly ideal, a false narrative. Who wrote the rule that says a man must have a woman to be successful? Or that if he's married, he's suddenly more put together, more reliable. Why do we trust men just because they have a woman at their side? Like it would be impossible for the devil to find a wife?

Clearly, society has some fucked up ideas.

He tugs me into the mansion, his fingers gripped around my wrist. I stare at the connection where his skin meets mine, a link so simple, and yet I can't break it.

Because I'm afraid of the consequences of letting go.

And truthfully, I don't know how to let go.

I've thought about it every day since Naz found me at Lily's grave. My mind has explored every option of walking away from my family, searching for any opportunity. But they would find me. I'm guarded in the house, can't leave on my own. I don't even have a car, never even learned how to drive.

I feel like a princess in one of those fairytales. One where they lock her away for too many years and by the time she's free she doesn't even know how to function. I was coddled, shielded, given too much. By the time I realized I was in a toxic relationship with my family, the threads had been wound too tightly.

The governor's wife smiles, her lips painted with a bright coral color. She wears a black dress and there's an elegant string of pearls wrapped around her throat. She looks every bit the perfect housewife. My google search this morning told me she's been married to the governor for nearly twenty years. They have two kids, a boy and girl, living the perfect American Dream.

"You must be Lana!" she coos sweetly, pulling me in for a hug. "I'm Diane. When Davis told us he was engaged, we just *had* to have you over."

She looks nice enough, but I have no interest in pretending to be civil to her. Nor do I want to celebrate this charade of an engagement. I give her a small smile and I feel Davis squeeze my hand. When my eyes dart to him he flashes me a dark look, his menacing gaze telling me to be nicer.

"Thank you," I tell Mrs. Bailey. "It's very nice of you to have us."

"Of course," she says, shaking my hand before ushering me further into the house. The movement forces Davis to drop his grip on me while he greets the governor. "Come on," she tells me, leading me toward the bar cart. "Wine?" she asks, her drawn on brow lifting with the question.

She grabs two glasses, filling each with more than one serving of red wine. Immediately she brings the glass to her lips, taking a gulp. I feel her character break for a moment, a crack in the facade, before just as quickly it's replaced.

I shake it off, letting her lead me over to the dining room. Davis eyes the glass of wine in my grip with a sore expression. I wonder what he'll do when he has me fully under his thumb? When I'm locked inside my new gilded cage? Will he punish me for this? Wrap his fingers around my throat again to assert his control?

NATALIA LOUROSE

My mind wanders through the possibilities, his abuse and control could be endless. I wonder at what point it will feel normal. Will I eventually not even flinch at his commands?

Naz's medal burns against my skin, making me painfully aware of the fact that I'm not with him.

There's a staff that serves dinner laying far too much food on the table for four people. My family has always hired employees, the only one who opposed it, was my grandmother. She was the type of woman who liked to do everything herself, my mother on the other hand was quick to hire help.

"So," Diane asks, finishing her wine, "how'd you two meet?"

I look to Davis to answer the question, not sure what kind of lie he'd like me to spin for people instead of the truth. We don't have a cute story, no one will smile upon hearing our meeting.

Well, I first saw him the night my sister jumped from her balcony. He came in to assess the damage before letting my parents know that I would be a suitable replacement. Oh, that's right, he was engaged to her first.

"Her family," he tells Diane, eyeing me over the rim of his bourbon glass, "I've known her family for a long time."

"Ah, well everyone knew Carmine Costello." The

mayor smiles as his gaze lands on me. "Which one of his daughters is your mother?" he asks.

People generally know my grandfather and Junior, but my mother and her sisters tend to get lost in the mix. Sad, really, how no one remembers the women in the family. This is a man's world, and the rest of us, those without a dick hanging between our legs seem to mean much less.

"Carlotta," I tell him.

"Ah," he snaps his fingers, "that's right, married Damien Romano." The way he spouts off my father's name only proves my point further.

Somehow, my gender has made me forgettable.

I zone out the dinner conversation, smiling and nodding and only speaking when someone asks me a question.

I watch as Diane refills her glass for the third time this evening, pouring the last drop into her cup. "Oops." She smiles. "Looks like we're all out. I'll run and get another." She's barely pushed herself out of the chair when the mayor's hand shoots over, pushing her back into her seat. The action happens so fast I barely catch it.

"No need, dear," he says, his voice sickeningly sweet. "I'm sure you've had enough."

Diane pales at his statement but nods her head,

her eyes looking down and away from her husband.

The whole thing sits poorly with me, like lead sinking in my stomach. Davis doesn't flinch, him and the mayor go right back to their conversation. Diane inhales a breath and turns back to me with a shaky smile.

My chest tightens and my ears block out whatever she says next.

My mind replays the scene in my head, only this time, it's me sitting in Diane's seat. I'm twenty years older, my bruises are hidden beneath expensive concealer and my children sit upstairs in their bedrooms. Do they have bruises too? My fingers itch for the wine glass, for the only thing that numbs the pain of being married to the man sitting next to me.

When I blink and Diane comes back into focus, I think I'll vomit. The quick visualization felt too real, too intense. The agony of the unhappiness settled into my bones. My feet feel glued to the floor, stuck in place.

I have the sudden urge to make it all stop.

I need to get the emotions out, need to let loose the anxiety that swirls in the pit of my stomach.

"Where's your bathroom?" I ask, but I can't hear the words that leave my lips. Diane's face looks concerned as she points down the hall. I don't hear whatever she says, the blood rushing through my head is too loud. I stumble as I stand, my heels slipping on the hardwoods. I rush to the bathroom, closing the door behind me and hurling myself toward the porcelain toilet.

I lose everything I just ate and when I finally finish, my face is sweaty and I feel exhausted.

"Lana," Diane's sweet voice coos as she knocks on the door. I crawl toward the gold handle, twisting the lock so she can open the door.

When it swings open, I see his face, a scowl etched across his features as he looks down at me on the bathroom floor. He pushes past Diane, bending down to be at eye level with me. "You're sick?" he asks, and I can't tell if it's concern that laces his tone or if he's disgusted with me.

"I'm sorry," I mutter, wiping the back of my hand across my lips.

He turns back to Diane. "I should get my fiancé home seeing as she's not feeling well."

I'm thankful for the wave of sickness if only because I can leave and let go of this facade, but I'm fearful to be alone with Davis. Especially now. I can feel the anger radiating from him and I think if he hits me, I'll die.

He leads me to the car, shutting me in before he

waves a final goodbye. "They'll think you're pregnant," he says once he slides into the driver's seat.

"I'm sorry," I whisper, pressing my head against the cold glass of the window.

"Are you?" he asks, his tone accusing.

Pregnant, he means. He wants to know if I'm pregnant. And considering he's never gotten me naked, he's afraid I have Naz's child inside me. I'm not.

"I have an IUD," I say, not bothering to look at him. The thing was a bitch to have put in.

"So you're not denying it?"

"Denying what?" I ask, finally lifting my head so I can look at him. His jaw is tight, his entire posture rigid.

"Did you sleep with him again, Lana?" he asks. "Or did you find someone else?"

"I don't' know—"

"Don't lie to me," he cuts me off as he turns the car onto the next street too quickly. The speed of the turn shoves me into the car door. He's being reckless. Davis has a bad habit of being unhinged around me.

"I haven't slept with him," I say, gripping onto the handle on the door frame. "But I figured you wouldn't believe me and it doesn't matter because I'm not pregnant."

He swerves again, the motion making my stomach churn.

"I swear to God, girl, if you're carrying his child" — his teeth clench — "I'll cut it out myself."

I believe him, which makes the threat that much scarier.

I don't know what to say to end this rage that's consuming him, what to do to make him not want to murder me. "I'm not," I whisper, and he doesn't respond, but he does slow the car down. I exhale with relief.

But inside, I'm still shaking.

I don't want this.

This fear, this scrutiny. I don't want to live like this.

Davis drives through the streets, taking me back to my house, and I can't get away from him fast enough. But I can count the weeks until our wedding on one hand, and my stomach revolts at the thought.

I can't fucking live like this.

I don't count the tablets of Advil before I tip back my head and drop the little red pills in my mouth. My eyes linger on the glass shelves in the medicine cabinet, looking for something else to take. Anything else to numb me, to silence the racing thoughts that fill my head.

I want a break.

Need a fucking break.

I can't handle the emotions that are competing with each other for first place. All the buildings are falling down around me, and I don't know where to run because nowhere is safe. I knock things off the shelves as I spin around bottles and push aside my beauty products. There's nothing good here, nothing to dull the edges.

I heave in another breath, my chest rattling with the action. Everything feels on fire. Everything's overwhelming.

And then in my head, I see Diane again, that split second where her face changed, realizing she had angered her husband. It was that flash, that quick moment, fear washed over her features. I saw it, the fear of what was to come next. What kind of hit, what kind of nasty words will he say to make you feel like nothing. And he will make her feel like nothing.

That's what men like him and Davis do. They sling the right words, the right hits, everything they do is aimed at controlling. At owning us.

I didn't need to see him hit her to know what thoughts spun through her head.

How many years has it been for her? How many bruises has she covered up? They have two kids. Two more people she has to protect, take care of all with that paralyzing fear.

I can't do that.

I can't get up every day, waiting for him to snap. His charming demeanor disappears alarmingly quick and he expects his every wish and whim to be followed. Where does that leave me?

No, I can't do that.

But I don't see a way out. The wedding is less than a month away. My parents are determined to make this happen, no matter how much I beg or try to talk to them. Hell, I sported his handprint on my neck for weeks, and they didn't give a shit.

Junior has made no move to stop them, and while I think my uncle is better than my parents, I can't be sure he's not okay with this plan.

They want this Alliance. Need another politician in their pocket.

I wish it weren't like this.

Lily flashes through my mind, images of her running along the edge of Grandfather's property. I'm behind her and she's reaching for me, trying to pull me along with her. I remember the day Dad was playing with us in the backyard. Mom watches from behind, a wide smile on her face.

The memory slows me down. I lean against the bathroom wall, letting my back slip down the surface.

It was good once.

Before.

For a moment when we were just a family.

No mafia. No politics. No plotting.

I can't pinpoint when it all stopped. When everything changed and I was no longer just a kid with a sister and happy parents. When did the smiling stop and the laughter end? There's no moment when I go from being that little girl who loved her family to the one who felt betrayed and alone.

But I know I can't be the dutiful daughter anymore.

I can't step into a life that I know will ruin me, break me beyond repair.

And maybe I'm not brave enough.

I don't think I believe that you only get what you can handle. I don't think that everything happens for a reason or that the sun will rise tomorrow.

I feel like the world is burning down around me and living another day with this fear, this fucking dread, isn't worth it at all.

I don't believe that there's a meaning to this, or that there is any point to being alive. I don't serve a purpose, there's no lesson to be learned from this.

And there's Lily, with her hand out, begging me to follow her.

I don't make the decision, don't think about what this means as I stand up. My feet just move, padding over the soft carpet and toward the hallway.

It's a sudden haze that comes over me as I go now, heading toward my parents' room. I feel warm and lighter for once. I find my mom's bathroom, opening her medicine cabinet and shifting the pill bottles. I land on the one I want, a bottle of klonopin. My mother isn't above antidepressants. I take the whole bottle, bringing it back to my room.

The warmth settles over me as I sit down on my bed with the pills and a bottle of water. I don't take them slowly, instead I tip the bottle back like it was a shot, alternating with chugs of water until I swallow every last one of the pills.

It feels dramatic.

And right.

And when I lay my head back onto my pillow, my eyes focused on my ceiling, I feel fine with the action.

Because this, all of this means nothing.

It's not until I feel that burn on my chest, and my hand reaches for the St. Jude medal, that I remember him. My fingers trace over the gold and my world begins to recolor itself, lighting up with the hues. It's as if for a moment I forgot about everything outside of the walls of my head. My mind was too busy imagining the worst things that were going to happen to me, spinning with tales of the misery I was soon to experience that I forgot.

But now, I see Naz in his apartment, standing over the stove, cooking the perfect grilled cheese. I imagine him in his bed, the sheet hanging barely above his hip bones. I can see that smile that rises on his cheeks when he laughs. I think of him on the rooftop patio, dark ink peeking from beneath his white t-shirt and the smile on his lips as he watches me smoke for the first time.

And I smile. Thinking of him, laughing.

That feeling, that happiness, that's what I want.

There's a lightness to it, as if my mind is free in those moments, no longer weighted down with the thoughts and feelings that invade me now. The chain to the anchor has snapped, releasing all the weight and letting me drift away.

I'm hazy, I realize, floating off into space right when I realize what I did.

How many pills did I swallow?

I spin on my stomach, using all the energy I have. I have to crawl to the edge of my bed, reaching for the drawer of my nightstand and the phone that sits inside it. I have to power it on and it feels like forever until I pull up his contact and press call.

When he answers, his voice is groggy; I think I woke him up.

"Naz," I whisper, and I feel lighter, softer, as if I could just let it all drift off.

"Lana, what's wrong?" He sounds worried.

"I think I made a mistake."

CHAPTER TWENTY-ONE

Naz

"WHAT HAPPENED?" I ASK, MY body shooting up into a sitting position. She sounds off, her voice is slowed and soft. She doesn't sound like her normal self. "Lana, did you take something?"

"Pills," she whispers and my heart stops beating in my chest. My lungs refuse to pull in oxygen. For just the briefest moment, I wonder if this is how Romeo felt before he licked the poison from Juliet's lips.

Why should I keep going if she's not here?

"Where are you?" Asking the question feels like a kick-start to my system. I can't fall back into that mindset, that darkness, because she's here right now. Her voice is on the other end of the phone and I need to find her. Need to stop this.

"Home," she breathes.

I don't think about what I'm doing as I slip on my jeans, a jacket, and shoes. Grabbing my car keys from the counter, I run to my car.

I keep her on the phone, making her talk to me through the Bluetooth speaker as I speed to her house.

I can't think about what I'm doing, I just have to keep moving, keep going toward her.

Her parents aren't there when I arrive, but she has guards, men trying to step in my path as I leap from my Jeep and run toward the door. It's Tony who's outside, looking at me with a confused expression.

"I need to see her," I shout, running up toward Tony's outstretched hands.

"What the fuck are you talking about, kid?" he asks.

"Lana, she tried to kill herself." Tony looks shocked, panic settling over his features. He spins, pushing open the door. I don't wait for an invitation, instead I rush forward pushing past him and treading up the stairs.

"Lana!" I call, I don't know which room is hers but I don't stop. I push open doors as I run down the hall until I finally find her. She's on her side on the bed, her eyes closed. If I didn't know, I would think she looked peaceful.

I pick her up in my arms and slide onto the bed, not slowing my pace. Keeping her on her side I lift her onto my lap, using one hand to pull open her mouth while I shove my fingers in her throat with the other.

"You don't get to give up on me, Lana. You don't get to be selfish and take the easy way out." I'm yelling and begging her to live at this point. She convulses beneath me and I turn her head to the side as she vomits, helping her get all the pills out.

"Good job, baby," I tell her, stroking her hair. I don't even pay attention to the vomit spilling over the bed. I just focus on her. Soothing her. Healing her.

And when it's all over, I lift up her limp body and carry her toward the shower. Tony tries to interject but I flip him off.

He's calling the Romanos, presumably telling them their daughter just tried to kill herself and the scum is here helping her.

I don't know what's going to happen next. How they'll handle this. Lana's clearly not okay, clearly not happy.

I help her strip off her dirty clothes, and I put her in the shower, rinsing her off. She lets me lead her through the motions, both of us quiet as we go. I get her dressed, pulling pajama pants up her legs and a t-shirt over her chest.

Tony only waits outside while she's undressed, clearly annoyed with the situation. I know there will be hell to pay when her parents get here, but I put off the worry, because whatever happens it was worth it to know she's okay.

"I'm okay," she whispers, crawling back into bed. "It was... I shouldn't have—"

"Shh." I sit down next to her, my heart rate finally slowing for the first time since I answered my phone. The digital alarm clock next to her bed reads 12:03. Her parents will come back soon, I'm sure, their Saturday night adventures cut short from Tony's call.

"I'm not weak," she breathes, the words light and fragile. "I'm *terrified*." The single word drips with vulnerability. I don't need to ask her to know why she's terrified. The bruises that coated her neck not long ago still live rent free in my mind.

She needs an out, an escape plan. Something to rid her of the chains that hold her here. I'm a second away from asking her to run, to leave with me when her bedroom door is swung open. My lips are parted, the words hanging on my tongue.

"You don't have to explain it to me," I whisper. And she doesn't. She doesn't owe me a damn thing. But I want her to live. Not for me, though. Not for these stolen moments or poorly kept secrets. I want her to live for herself. I wish she wanted to get up in the morning, her head filled with plans and dreams for the future. I want her to live because she loves it.

Not for anyone else.

Just for herself.

Her fingers find the charm dangling from her throat and I watch as she delicately brushes her thumb over the metal. "That night..." She trails, her eyes avoiding mine. "Why...why were you there?" As she whispers the question her gaze comes back to mine and I can see the pain that sits there, lingering in her hazel eyes.

I can't imagine what it's like to be her. I've had this image of her family in my head for years, this idea that money just automatically makes everyone happy and that there were no exceptions. But I can see now how I was. Money hasn't made Lana happy, it's only built a cage around her.

I don't want to answer her question, because I know it won't solve anything for her. It won't give her closure or make anything better.

"Lana..." I don't know how to say the words, my voice breaking as I say her name. I scrub a hand over my face. "I moved her body." The words feel heavy on my tongue, wrong.

"I never understood," she whispers, "why everyone thought she was in the Quarter that night."

"Marcus had me move her, your father didn't want the police in the house."

She laughs, a rough sound, not at all the melodic one I'd become used to. "Sounds right," she says. "*Asshole.*"

"Lana!" Her mother's voice is a high-pitched screech, wailing through the room, and suddenly I'm transported to the last time I was in this mansion, to the night her sister jumped off the balcony.

I was with Marcus when he had gotten the call, dropping off a wad of cash. He had sighed heavily in response to the news given over the phone. Then he hung up and his eyes landed on me. "You want to earn your place in this family?" He had asked me in only the way that powerful men do, like there is an option associated with their question when we both know that the only acceptable answer is yes.

So I nodded my head.

The job was a cleanup. The Romanos, despite the fact their daughter had just committed suicide, didn't want cops at their house. So we moved the body, me and another man from Marcus's crew. We scrubbed any trace of her from the concrete beneath her balcony and moved her to a club outside of the Quarter, tossing her body from a third floor patio and paying the owner off.

Money in the right hands can make most sto-ries stick and within a week the cops were leaving Damien Romano alone, giving him space to grieve.

What kind of parents do this to their children? Making them so miserable to the point of not wanting to live. And then moving her body so they don't have to accept any blame for their actions.

There's a part of me, a naive child, that thinks they'll call it off. That one death and scare is enough. But then again, I think I know something Lana doesn't.

That this deal is more than just an *alliance* between two powerful families. Underneath the image and connections there's a business deal that's been wait-ing for years to be made.

Damien reaches for the collar of my shirt, pulling me off the bed and away from his daughter. "You," he growls, the words coated with venom as if I'm the one who hurt his daughter.

He didn't need any help with that.

"What did you do to her?" he asked, slamming my spine against her bedroom wall. "She was fine until you showed up. Fucking *trash*," he snarls.

My eyes coat with red, blurring my vision. Com-pared to him, I'm a fucking angel. A pure, heavenly angel. I'll never be like him, I would never put my child in the position that he put Lana in. Anger boils in my veins at his words.

I'm not the villain here.

I push back, using my forearm against his chest and spin him around. I shove his back against the wall, pinning my arm to his neck as I push down.

"Me?" I growl. "This was all you, Damien. What did you think would happen when you sold her off to that psychopath? You thought she'd dance off into the sunset?" I press harder on his throat, the anger making me reckless.

The only thing to pull me out of my tunnel vision is Lana's sad cry from behind me. "Stop."

I ease my grip on Damien and he uses the advantage, pushing me off him. "Ya little prick."

"Stop," Lana yells again. "I'm fine, it's not his fault."

Damien doesn't look happy as he straightens out his shirt. "You better get the fuck out of my house." He angles his jaw toward the door, his eyes locked on me.

I can't leave her here. I don't trust them, and I don't know where Lana's head is right now. What will happen if I abandon her with these two?

"It's okay, Naz," she says and smiles weakly. "I

promise you, I'm fine. I won't mess up again." She's staring at me deeply, trying to convey a message through her eyes. Saying *don't worry about me.* But the thing is, I can't stop worrying about her. She's the only place I've felt safe, somewhere I could call home. With her, I could finally breathe. If only for a moment.

And I would do anything to get back to that moment, of happiness and *relief.*

I want her eyes to tell me that we'll get there. That this is just a roadblock in our path together.

I can't be sure, but I don't see any other options.

I nod my head, hoping in that simple movement I can actually display what I'm feeling. Begging that she can see how much I want tomorrow with her. Pray that she knows I'm addicted to her, and I want to see every day of her life until she's old and gray. That I can't bear the thought of never seeing her smile again. And she won't smile today, but maybe someday, and I'm clinging on to that.

The words don't come out. Not with Damien and Carlotta's gazes glued to me. So instead, I hope my eyes say it, hope she gets it and understands.

Every fiber of my being hurts at the thought of leaving her here, my soul on fire. But she nods back, telling me to go.

So I do.

No one stops me as I walk through the hall; Tony only gives me a curt nod as I leave the house.

I slam the door of my Jeep, my whole body throbbing from the pain of leaving her behind after knowing what she just did. Leaving her in the hands of those people.

There must be something I can do, something more. But I can't think of a better plan as I pluck my phone from my pocket and pull up Sam's contact.

It's time he lets me in on his plan.

Leaving Lana behind has me feeling empty. I tossed and turned all night, my heart aching inside my chest. It felt like someone had wrapped their fingers around the organ and squeezed tightly.

I've never felt this way about someone, never gave someone enough of my heart to feel like this.

I was guarded — protected myself — before her. I can't place what it is about her that made me so damn vulnerable, willing to risk everything for her.

Even as I drive my Jeep across town, my eyes roaming the rearview mirror in search of followers, it's not me that I'm worried about.

My mind is racing with thoughts of what her family might do to her.

The only thing I do know, is that they have no intention of helping her.

I find Sam at his apartment, a million-dollar historic townhouse in the French Quarter. My mind is racing with the combination of anger and guilt. I'm not sure if I want to punch Sam or pray he has a solution, the endgame in sight.

"What happened?" he asks, his palms are sprawled across his oak desk. His office sits on the second floor of his home, the windows looking out into the quarter.

Frown lines mar his face, and for a second I think that Sam might be the only one is his finally trying to protect Lana as much as I am.

I scrub a hand over my face before I answer his question. I'm exhausted, my bones aching, my head throbbing. "She tried to kill herself."

"How?"

"Pills." I blow out a breath. "She swallowed a bunch of pills." My stomach twists as I tell him.

Sam exhales heavily when he runs a hand through his hair. "Damnit," he growls, slamming his hand down on the desk. "They're gonna fucking kill her, both of them with their antics."

"They?" I ask. Sam shifts his gaze to me at the question.

"Damien and Carlotta, the two cunts. I didn't want Lana to...follow in her sister's footsteps." He sounds remorseful when he says it, and it's the first time I've heard him mention his other cousin.

To be fair, all of New Orleans stopped talking about Lily a week after her suicide. It was like the whole town forgot about the dead Costello grandchild. But I kept seeing her mangled body in my dreams. Even though I'd never met the girl, only knew her by the status associated with her. Still, I drove three miles with her body in the trunk of my car. It was enough to make her memorable.

It was a new kind of fucked-up for me.

But the money...it always came back to the money.

It always came back to Ma, Elly, and Anthony.

I would steal, sell drugs, and move dead bodies as long as the three of them were safe and happy.

"Why?" I ask him, annoyance lacing my tone. "Why are they doing this? What's so important about LaFontaine anyway?"

Sam's eyes lift to mine, and there's a look on his face, something I can't quite place. I think he's measuring me up, wondering if he should really tell me.

"Hold on," he says, and he opens his desk drawer. He pulls out a stack of cards, plopping them down on the walnut surface, next a knife, and finally a lighter. "You want this?" he asks, his eyes meeting mine, holding my gaze as if he can tell by just the look in my eyes if I'm lying.

"Yes," the words leave me in a hushed whisper.

This is what I want. What I've been working for.

"One more question," Sam asks, spinning the lighter between his fingers. "Are you doing this for you or *her?*"

I only think about his question for a moment. Is this for me or Lana? "Why can it be both?" I tell him.

A sly grin lifts the corner of his lips. "It can. Pick a saint, Naz." He pushes the cards toward me and when I flip the stack over in my palm, the first one to look at me is St. Jude. His pale face stares up at me, green fabric draped over his shoulder and a staff rests in his palm.

I pick his card up, holding eye contact with the picture of the saint that has guided me from childhood.

Even if I claimed that I didn't believe in religion, even having never prayed to God, I have always prayed to Saint Jude, rubbing my fingers over the gold metal.

The patron saint of lost causes.

It's fitting really that he would be the saint I take from this deck, that he would be the one to usher me into this position even when I stand here without the medal wrapped around my throat.

I set the rest of the cards down, showing Sam that I've made my pick.

"Saint Jude." He smiles. "Sounds about right." Sam lifts the knife from his desk, shifting the blade in his hand before he looks back to me. "We're doing this without the fanfare. It's normally a bigger deal."

I've heard through whispers about the initiation. Normally they drag you to a building with a hood over your head, spouting off about loyalty and family while holding you at gunpoint, or at least that's what the rumors say.

Sam gestures for me to give him my hand and I do. He uses the knife to slice a line through my palm, letting red blood pool in the wound. Next, he hands me the lighter. "Burn the card in your hand."

I flick the lighter on and bring the flame to the St. Jude card, watching as the flame grabs onto the paper, trickling over the ink and the face of my chosen saint. "Repeat after me," Sam says. "If I betray my friends or family, I and my soul will burn in hell like this saint."

ALLIANCE

I repeat the words, my oath to this family, to this organization that's built me. This is what I've been working for, this is what I've wanted.

But as the flames reach my fingertips and the fire burns my flesh, I don't feel like I have succeeded. I still feel like I'm playing with fire, and when you play with fire you'll always get burned. I drop the burning card into the bowl Sam gives me. We both watch as the card burns out, leaving a pile of ash in the stone bowl.

"You're a part of this now," Sam says, clapping a hand on my shoulder. "You're a brother, a made man. You work for me, understood?"

I nod my head and Sam drops his hand from my shoulder, wiping his palms down his dress pants before he moves back to his desk.

"Just one little task force that needs to be disassembled and money will be flowing into their pockets," he says.

"What are you talking about?"

Sam gestures for me to sit down across from him, so I do. He sighs heavily as he tells me.

"Davis has an in with the mayor, and my uncle has a new money maker he's trying to implement. The problem is, this task force keeps catching his men, keeps stopping him before he can get the prod-

251

uct into the States."

"What product?" I ask.

Sam looks away and I realize he doesn't want to answer me, even with the burning flesh on my finger-tips, there are still things he doesn't want to tell me.

"So what?" I ask. "They want Lana to marry Davis so he disassembles a task force?"

Sam nods, leaning forward with his elbows on his desk. "There's a lot of money at stake here and money makes people do crazy things."

"He gets a cut?" I ask.

"Yep. He gets a cut, and the marriage solidifies everyone's loyalty. As long as Davis is married to her, he'll be considered family. That's what they want, an unbreakable alliance that will fill their pockets and keep the business running."

"Even if she's unhappy."

Sam scoffs. "They don't care if she's happy, Naz. They care about two things only. Money and power, and let me tell you from experience, one leads to the other."

I wonder if Lana knows that her family has assigned a dollar amount to her worth.

The marriage is an unnecessary part, a silly symbol meant to strengthen their deal. But this could easily be done without hurting her, not that anyone will acknowledge that. Instead, they'll force her into this marriage, calling on old traditions while Lana is swirling in thoughts of death.

It's stupid. And I want to kill all of them for it. For putting her through this.

And maybe I'm weak for not killing them right here and now, but where would that get me? There's no way in hell I'd make it out of this house.

"So what are we going to do about it?" I cross my arms as I meet Sam's gaze.

There was a war brewing in New Orleans long before I got wrapped up in the Costello business. But now? Now I was choosing a side. Lana's side.

Sam's phone buzzes on the table, and he reaches for it, bringing the device to the ear and growling a greeting. The frown on his face only grows as he listens to the caller on the other end. "What the fuck are you talking about?"

I can hear a pounding on his door at the same time when Sam is yelling at the voice on the other end. An incessant beating, banging loudly from downstairs.

"Fuck," he growls, and the change of the tone make my stomach drop.

Whatever's happening, I can tell it's not good.

I step back to the window, peeking out of the blinds to look down at the entrance to Sam's house.

"Police," I say the word as I look down at the black uniformed officers standing outside his door.

"Shit," Sam mutters, pulling the phone from his ear and jabbing at the red button to end the call.

"What is it?"

Sam weaves a hand through his hair in frustration.

"My father is dead."

It's not until this moment that I realize how entwined I am in the Costello family. Before this, I considered myself nothing more than just an employee. But as Sam readies himself for the police to arrest him, he tells me, "Don't trust anyone but John. Wait for him to contact you."

It's those words that make me realize how deep I am. The understanding that whatever is happening in this family that is tearing them apart, is more than just Lana's marriage.

There's no secret that there's a divide straight down the line between the older and younger Costello children. But the way Sam warns me who not to trust reinforces the idea that something is happening in this family.

Lana is just the tipping point.

Sam is cuffed on the front stop of his home. He holds out his hands for the officers to take him into custody. They take down my name but leave me behind. If I wasn't connected to *La famiglia* before, I definitely am now.

And I finally have my button, the thing I've been working for, but I feel less protected now than I did a year ago.

Sam's parting words to me are "Protect Lana."

What was missing from the sentence was how the fuck I was going to do that.

Junior Costello being dead really fuck things up. Not to mention, the charges read while they slapped handcuffs on Sam's wrists had me believing he was being charged for his father's murder.

I guessed that leaves Damien a lot of time to take over the family while Sam is busy battling murder charges.

I don't have a plan now. I leave Sam's house with more questions than answers. Lana's wedding is in a few weeks and with Sam behind the bars, what kind of pull do I have to protect her or end this arrangement?

And waiting for John to contact me? How long am I supposed to sit around while some asshole wraps his fingers around her neck? Tortures her to the point of swallowing a bottle of sleeping pills?

I slam my fist into the dashboard of my Jeep,

screaming out the pent-up frustration.

How the fuck am I going to fix this one?

CHAPTER TWENTY-TWO

Lana

THREE DAYS. SEVENTY-TWO HOURS. THAT'S how much freedom I have left.

After those three days, those sweet seventy-two hours, Lana Romano will cease to exist. In her place will be Mrs. LaFontaine, likely to be a miserable bitch.

I'm holding on. Only because Naz asked me to, though. My mind keeps wandering back to the fuzzy memories of drifting off. There's a pang of guilt that hits my gut, wrecking me, but only in association to Naz. If it weren't for him I probably would have let myself drift into the abyss.

Even though my mother was quick to correct me after the attempt. Google told her that pills weren't an effective method of suicide. So even in my attempted death, I failed.

My parents didn't handle the whole thing well. Since that day I've been carefully watched. My mother doesn't leave me alone, for the first time in my life, she's attentive to me. Stalking me like a child who's incapable of taking care of herself. The sudden attention has only made me feel suffocated.

She follows me everywhere, constantly spending time with me under the pretense that she'll miss me when I move in with Davis but I think we both know that's a lie.

What's worse is the secrecy around it. My parents refused to tell Davis what I did and limited my communication with the outside world as if that would suddenly make me *better*. I think in reality they're embarrassed, ashamed of having two daughters who would rather die than live with them.

"This is nice," Ma says, bringing her glass of diet coke to her lips. Diet coke because she won't drink her normal glass of wine in front of me anymore. Tonight's dinner at a restaurant in the Quarter was only because guilt had been gnawing at her.

She presented the idea to me this morning as a sort of last night out before marriage. I asked if she meant a *bachelorette party* and she frowned. I don't think she likes to be reminded that I'm unhappy. She's concocted her own reality where she believes this is okay and that I'm not slowly dying beside her.

I've concluded that's how she does it. She disassociates so well she doesn't even realize half the time. She's so damn focused on *winning*, on being better than her siblings that she has forgotten anything else exists.

Jealousy hits me. I wish I could live in my own dream world where none of this exists.

"Yep." I'm not interested in small talk while I sit with my mother, stabbing at the green leaves on my plate.

It's perfect timing really, the group of girls laughing loudly as they enter the restaurant. In the middle is a twenty-something girl with a tiara and a white veil. Her body is sheathed in a white bodycon dress with high heels. She's surrounded by girls, chatting and smiling.

A chill slides down my arms as the heaviness settles in my chest, the weight crushing me. I can't have that. No group of friends. No drunken debauchery. No night out.

Instead I'll have surveillance as I count down the days until my pending marriage.

There's a buzz running through my body, sounding loudly in my brain. I can't focus on anything else but the bachelorette party, not my mother with her wedding talk, not the food on my plate, *nothing*. I'm overwhelmed with the ache in my heart, the sadness that has overtaken me.

I've run out of options and it's slowly eating away at me.

I shouldn't have called Naz. I think I should have just let myself drift away. But that line of thought makes me spiral again. I can remember the look on his face as he ran his fingers through my hair, holding me close to his chest. He was *devastated*.

If Davis wasn't so damn controlling I would consider marrying him for appearances only and sneaking off with the man I truly loved, but I know that won't work. My future husband wants to control everything.

I heave a breath, the anxiety welling up in my chest, and Carlotta gives me a sharp look.

She's waiting for me to break, I think. Waiting for me to shove pills down my throat or find a more effective method. Her eyes dig into mine, looking for a sign, something to warn her of the incoming storm.

I can feel the beginning of it, the breakdown that's coming for me and I know she can too.

Both of us know you can't survive and not change a damn thing.

All of the feelings, all of the moments that lead me to downing the pill bottle like a shot of liquor are still there, lingering in the background noise.

My parents haven't changed.

Davis hasn't changed.

And neither have I.

Escaping isn't easy.

I feel like a conspiracy theorist as I map out my escape plan in the walls of my mind. Looping strings around red pins and staring at my masterpiece, even if it's just an idea in my head.

First, I ask to visit Lily's grave, something my mother won't deny me but also won't join me for. Ma doesn't visit Lily's tomb; to do so, she would need to deconstruct the fictional universe that she's created. She'd need to admit that her oldest daughter killed herself to escape, and she won't do that.

So she waves her hand, telling Tony to take me.

The next step is leaving Tony in the car, which is easy. Tony, having known Lily since she was a child, also hates visiting her tomb. It makes it too real for him, and so he sits in the car while I enter the cemetery.

Being out of his watch gives me the opportunity I need. I leave my phone tucked into the backseat and head for Lily's tomb. I have to walk past it quickly, trying not to look or else I'll spend too much time talking to her, and she can't help me now.

My sister, my best friend, is gone. And I'm learning that I need to pick, I can either be alive and live in the moment or I can live in the cemetery, clinging to the past. But I don't think I can have both. I can't live with one foot already in the grave.

I give her tomb a wistful glance as I pass.

I walk to the back, to the other side where Naz entered that day weeks ago. I pat myself on the back for the foresight to wear sneakers and athletic pants. It doesn't take much effort for me to climb over the gate. And then I'm off. Running toward the bus station. There's enough cash in my pocket for me to pay the fare. I didn't bring a credit card because I don't have my own money and I don't want to be tracked. Instead, I broke my childhood piggy bank and freed a handful of cash.

The bus drops me off a block away from Naz's apartment, so I walk the rest of the way, checking over my shoulder to make sure no one's following me.

I hit the buzzer for his unit multiple times, pounding on the thing incessantly before I hear his deep voice growl through the speakers.

"It's me," I whisper, my voice coming out so soft, the words broken.

The door makes a clicking noise as it unlocks and I push it open. Naz is waiting for me when I reach his floor, his hand resting on the frame of the door. His shirt is already off, the black swirling ink on display. Black stubble covers his jaw, it's longer than normal and less neat, like he's forgotten to trim it. Strands of hair fall over his eye, and I wonder if he's stopped taking care of himself since that night.

Since I called him in the minutes after my attempt.

It takes him a moment before he remembers to let me in, like his brain has stopped working as he stands in the doorway, staring at me. He blinks hard and moves aside, making room for me. Maybe he's weighing the consequences of letting me cross that threshold. Another mistake. Another moment where he risks his life. And we both know that there's no happily ever after for us. That dream has long passed.

Inked fingers reach out to me in what feels like slow motion. My heart beats in my chest at an agonizingly slow pace, the thrumming rhythm holding me hostage. His thumb trails across my cheekbone and his dark eyes hold me in their gaze.

I feel a warmth wash over my body, a sense of comfort I've never experienced before. Before him. Everything is before and after Naz. Before my world was turned upside down, my body opened up and turned inside out. Back then, I was someone different, someone docile in her cage. Now I'm the tiger that paces the fence, searching for a way out. For freedom.

"Let's pretend." I wet my lips. "That nothing outside these four walls exists."

His eyes sparkle in the dim lighting of his apartment. "Nothing except us, huh?"

I can't help the smile that spreads across my lips as I listen to his answer. Nothing but us, I think that sounds perfect. "Yeah," I say.

The door shuts and his hands find me before the lock latches. His fingers trail over my skin, leaving goosebumps in their wake. Sweet kisses are pressed to my neck, his lips soft against my flesh. His body presses me back against the kitchen counter, the warmth envelopes me, casting a safety net over my body.

For once, I feel protected, washed in warmth and light.

"I'm still mad at you," he tells me, nipping at the spot where my neck and my shoulder meet. "You can't do that to me, baby, you can't scare me like that."

"I'm sorry," I whisper, meeting his lips with my own, kissing him in a way I hope portrays my apology, whispering the words that only my soul knows. Displaying my love for him.

"I need you to promise me, baby, I need you to promise me that you'll never give up. You'll never try to leave this world again. Because you, Lana Romano, are everything to me. I know that you'll never be mine, that I can't have you, but I don't care. I will love you through every second. No matter whose ring sits on your finger or whose last name is on your mailbox, you will always be mine."

I want to push away the tears that threaten to blur my eyes. There's a weight that sits on my chest, crushing me. My lungs tighten, fighting to pull in every breath, but even with that looming feeling, I can feel the warmth on my skin. Sunshine radiates from Naz, his warmth addictive. He feels like pure light.

I live for these moments. These stolen kisses and seconds of passion. His fire matches mine, the flames dancing along my flesh, captivating me in the best possible way.

I want to burn in this moment forever, my heart and my soul belongs to him, but I know my body doesn't. My hand, my life, was promised to someone else.

No matter how many roots Naz plants in my soul, no matter how much my heart begs for his touch. I still don't belong to him.

"No," I whisper, shaking my head at the same time. "There's a life for you after me. There's a wife and a family and normalcy. There is happiness out there for you, and you deserve it, every fucking second of this." My fingers grip onto his shoulders and a lone tear falls down my cheek. "Take it, please take it. Don't wait for me. Don't love me."

"Lana—"

"Shh," I whisper. "You can't fix me, Naz, you can't rescue me like a princess in a fucking tower. You can't make this go away. I'm not a project for you. You can't solve this.

"We can either take the moments we get, or we can have nothing. And I'll take the moments, every fucking second I can get with you. So I'm right here, right now. What happens tomorrow, we can deal with it then." The words fly from my mouth in a flurry.

And at that, his mouth crashes down on mine, devouring me. I can't get his clothes off fast enough, removing my hands from his skin feels impossible.

Sparks race through my body, every nerve ending on fire.

I ache for his touch, my body shaking as his hands work my shirt up, he breaks our kiss only to pull the material over my head. I unbutton his jeans, tugging the rough denim down.

I drop to my knees for him, wanting to worship every inch of his skin. He slides his boxers down, freeing his cock from the material. I wrap my hand around his width, stroking the velvet smooth skin as I bring my lips to his head.

I lick a drop of pre-cum as I lap my tongue over his shaft. Groans echo above me as his hand tangles into my hair. I smile against him, loving the sounds he makes as I take him further.

"Fuck, baby," he moans, his breath hitching as he watches me. His hand finds my face and pulls me back. "I should be taking care of you, pretty girl." His whisper is soft and sweet as he strokes his thumb along my cheeks.

"No, use me. Fuck me like he never will. Make me forget anyone else even exists."

His eyes darken at my words, but I know he feels it too. This primal need surging between us. His hand grips the base of my neck as he pulls me up, crashing his lips against mine.

He spins me around quickly, pushing me down onto the table so my ass is propped up. He rips me leggings down my legs, barring me to him. His hands wander over my skin, warming every inch of me as they move.

"Don't tell me what to do." His hand slaps against my ass, not hard enough to hurt me but enough to leave a dull sting. "If I want to fucking worship you" — he leans in, his breath skating across my skin — "I'll fucking worship you."

His knees drop to the floor behind me, and he spreads my legs further. Warm breath blows across my hot center. I'm aching for his touch, begging for his mouth on my most sensitive parts.

His tongue finds my center, spreading me open and drawing lazy circles over the bundle of nerves. He pulls back with a moan. "Fuck, baby, I forgot how good you tasted." My body burns at the dirty words, a shade of pink blooming across my chest.

I blush at his admission, but he doesn't slow down, he finds the sensitive spot again. Driving me wild with his merciless torture.

My legs shake, my body going weak. My fingers grip onto the edge of the table and I know I'm about to come, about to fall over the edge. His fingers grip onto my thighs steadying me from the fall I anticipate any time now.

There's a weightlessness to the pleasure, it feels

like I'm flying, the wind whipping at my skin. And then suddenly the fall starts, coming down from the high.

"We're not done yet." Naz's lips find their way back to my ears as he whispers, his warm breath sending a new round of sparks through my body.

He stands up, lining his cock up with my now soaked entrance. He pushes in effortlessly. Hands find their way to my hair, wrapping the locks around his fingers and pulling back just enough that I turn my head to look at him.

"You're fucking beautiful, baby. Do know that?" His eyes lock with mine. "Absolutely gorgeous," he continues. "You deserve to be fucking worshipped. You deserve to be treated like a queen. I don't care who you think you belong to, whose money fills your purse, whose DNA runs through your body—those people mean nothing to me. You? You, Lana Romano, mean everything."

I don't even realize I'm crying until he drops my hair, reaching his hand forward to wipe a tear from my eye. His body presses against mine, his skin warm and comforting. He trails kisses along my shoulder and over my cheekbone.

My body is on fire, my soul ignited by his words.

When I crash over the edge of my orgasm this time

there's no darkness, no shame of guilt lingering from the action. I fall right into the sun, warmth enveloping me. I don't know how loud I scream or how many times I chant his name while the waves of warmth wash over me. But when I open my heavy eyelids and steady my breathing, Naz is gasping above me, reeling from his own orgasm.

He lifts me up, carrying me over to the bed and laying me down with a kind of gentleness I've never known.

Happiness settles over me as he crawls into bed behind me, pressing his body firmly behind mine.

I want him to let me go. To move on and find someone better. Someone safer. That can love him and cherish him the way he deserves.

"You should go," I whisper, even though the words make my heart ache, feeling like it's shattered into a million pieces.

"Shut up." He presses a kiss to the back of my head. "I'm not going anywhere. You can't get rid of me that easily."

For a moment, a single second, a picture of our future flickers through my head. An image of him, a big house, screaming kids. Just a quick glimpse, a short picture of what could be.

I curl into him, soaking up his warmth. He should

go, or I should leave him alone, end whatever's happening between us. I try to push the idea of a future together from my head.

But I know I won't.

I won't push him away.

I live for these borrowed moments, these seconds where we pretend that nothing exists but us.

I'm covered in his fire.

He lit a match and everything around me was set ablaze. I can't go back to normal, I can't pretend that everything is okay.

I can't give up Ignazio Vaccola.

And I don't want to.

CHAPTER TWENTY-THREE

Naz

MA SETS A LOADED PLATE of food in front of me. Spaghetti piled high and a chicken cutlet, everything covered in her famous sauce. Normally her cooking has my mouth watering but today my stomach clenches.

"Ignazio?" Her hands smack the bony sides of her hips. "What's wrong, why do you look like that?"

I frown at the comment, at the insinuation that something about my appearance looks out of the ordinary. Though, she may be on to something. I feel less okay today, less put together. My clothes look more wrinkled than normal, my body aches, and my shoulders roll forward.

"What's wrong, Uncle Naz?" Anthony slurps a noodle through his lips before he asks the question.

There's a bit of red sauce smeared on his lips and he looks at me with innocent, naive eyes.

What's wrong? What's wrong is that my chest aches and my head won't stop spiraling with the idea of Lana being pushed around, used as a punching bag while I sit here enjoying dinner.

I flash back to my childhood, and instead of Anthony across from me, it's Elly, and there's no food smeared on her face, just an empty plate in front of her. Ma sets down a casserole dish, inside is some grayish sauce with spiral noodles. The top is sprinkled with crushed potato chips, probably that half a bag Elly brought home from a friend's house.

Elly turns her nose up, sniffing and pulling her head back quickly. "Ew!" she shouts. "What's that?" she asks.

Ma sighs. "Tuna noodle casserole."

Dad left three nights ago with the car. Ma hasn't left the house in those three days. Normally, she goes grocery shopping on Saturdays. It's Monday, but the fridge is still empty, the pantry bare. I don't want to ask. I think she prides herself on us not noticing. Not realizing that we're poor and Dad is gone for fuck knows how long.

She's scraped up whatever was left in the pantry. Tuna, ninety-nine cent noodles, a can of soup, and potato chip crumbs. My stomach clenches.

The food in front of me now is so different. There's so much more of it, the ingredients newer, better. So much has changed, and money did all of that.

I can't worry myself about where the money came from, what hands it was traded through before it landed in my pocket. All that matters is that it's here. That it put food on the table, kept the water flowing through our pipes. Money changes everything. A fact my family refuses to acknowledge.

Elly comes out from the hallway, plopping down at the end of the table. "Looks great, Ma."

Ma mumbles a self-deprecating thank you before untying her apron and sitting at the other end of the table.

"So," Elly starts, a slight smile etched on her lips, a pink color to her cheeks. "I have news." Her eyes look to me. "I got a new job."

"That's great," I tell her. My sister has been trying different jobs for years. She was a barista, a cashier, parked cars at the airport—a little bit of everything. "Where at?" I ask, spiraling the noodles around my fork.

"It's in New York," she says softly, her eyes watching for my reaction.

New York.

New York City?

Why the hell would my sister accept a job in New York? Anthony's only ten, she wants to move him that far away from Ma, from me?

"What?" I choke on the noodle I had just brought to my mouth. "What are you talking about?"

"We're moving," she says. "I accepted the job and we're moving in two weeks."

"You can't just move." I don't mean to yell or slam my fist down on the table until it's already done. All three faces look back at me with shock.

"No." Elly steels her spine. My sister has never been a pushover, she's always walked to the beat of her own drum. But I've always been there for her, always been two steps ahead of her, clearing the debris from the path. I didn't want her to struggle, not like we did when we were kids. "This is a done deal. I made my decision."

I wanted my family to have safety, security. I wanted to see food on our tables, roofs over our heads. And damn did I work for it. Worked my ass off to pay for this life.

And she's going to leave.

"Why?" I growl the question at her.

Her lips are pursed thin, and she crosses her arms when she looks at me. "Because I need a change of scenery, and honestly maybe you do too."

"What does that mean?"

"Look at yourself!" she yells back at me.

"Anthony" — Ma stands — "let's go get dessert ready." Anthony looks down at his half-full plate, then between me and his mother before he finally stands and nods his agreement.

Elly sighs heavily but as soon as they leave her mouth opens back up, ready to resume her argument. "Who are you? You run all over this city doing God knows what for who? For the Costellos? For the mob? What do you think that's going to do for you? I have a chance to start a new life, Naz. I want that and you can't stop me."

She talks about my job like she knows what I'm doing, but she doesn't. She has no idea about the work I put into this. The sacrifices I made. "And you're going to take Anthony?"

"Yes."

My heart aches at that. I've helped her raise that kid since the day he was born. Hell, I held her hand in the hospital while trying to avoid seeing where the kid came from.

I never loved a child until he was born.

"Elle—"

"No" — she waves her hand dismissively — "I

don't tell you want to do, and you can't tell me." She inhales deeply, soothing the anger that seeps from her before she continues, "I know you think you're doing the right thing. At least, I truly think you believe that. But you don't need to. Don't give up your life for us, don't nail yourself to a cross because you think it's what you need to do to save us. We don't need saving, Naz. And don't take that as I don't appreciate everything you've done for me, for Anthony. We love you so much." She pauses, dabbing at her eye to catch the tear that threatens to fall. "But I need to do this on my own. I need to be my own person and I can't do that in this city, not with all the baggage lying around." She gives me a meek smile.

I don't know what to say, don't know how to tell my baby sister that I can't handle her leaving. I can't comprehend the idea that she doesn't need me. My identity has been crafted around being the provider. Taking care of them.

But they don't want that anymore.

So who am I without my family?

"Do you remember it?" My voice cracks when I ask the question.

"Remember what?"

"Being poor," I whisper. "Starving, being cold, just…do you remember it?"

Elly thinks for a moment, tears glistening in her eyes. "I remember building a fort in the living room, lighting the place up with all of Ma's candles. I remember you giving me your sleeping bag so I'd be warm enough." She smiles thoughtfully. "And I remember how everything was game. Somehow you made it fun. Like how many peas can we find in the tuna noodle casserole? Or who can chug water from the sink faster?" She chuckles. "I never felt poor. We were different, sure. Other kids had things we didn't, but I never felt less than."

I can see the sincerity in her eyes, and it cracks my already shattered heart.

She reaches forward, grabbing my hand into her own. "I never needed the money, Naz," she whispers. "I never needed money, I just needed my big brother."

And with those words, the facade I've built comes crumbling down. Bits and pieces crashing around me. Tears fall from my eyes. I can't even remember the last time I've cried or the last time I've felt vulnerable.

My fingers itch to touch the worn gold St. Jude medal, but there's nothing there. Nothing hanging from my neck. I gave my comfort item away to protect someone else, the only thing I had to give her. I don't have the money to save her. The money that would make a worthwhile alliance for her family.

But I have me.

And maybe that's enough.

I don't think of my father often. I've shoved all of my memories of him into a box, securing the whole thing with a duct tape and pushing it as far back into my mind as I possibly can.

I don't like to think of him.

But my conversation with Elly sliced through the layers of tape, letting the lid to the box pop open and all of the memories burst free.

I can't stop now.

My mind runs through images of him. Hitting my mother. Stealing the little money we had. Once my grandma gave me a crisp five dollar bill for helping her in the garden. I hid it in my underwear drawer. It was like my father could sniff out the green cash, because the next day it was gone.

He was always high on something, always had some sort of drug coursing through his veins. He never noticed when the power was off or if there was no food in the pantry. He rarely ate, so I assume that bit didn't bother him much. He was mostly gone, and when he wasn't, he was either sleeping off whatever flowed through his system or screaming at us.

We never knew what to expect. We were constantly on edge, wondering if he'll come home that day, and if he would, what sort of mood would he be in?

There were good memories too, just far and few between.

One time, he took me to a baseball game. I don't remember how we got the tickets, but I remember sitting in the stands with him. We were far from the field, high up, way in the back, but it didn't matter much to me. He explained everything that was happening on the field, all of the rules of the game.

It felt different. Like he loved me and wanted to spend time with me.

I was on cloud nine when we left the game, my small body buzzing with excitement.

And then we stopped in the parking lot, my father pulling a few bills from his pocket and handing them off to someone. In exchange, they place a small bag of white powder in his hand.

That was the thing with my father. Even the good memories are tainted with drugs.

The first time Marcus handed me drugs to sell, I wanted to vomit. I hated the idea of selling the substance that my father was hooked on. At that point I hadn't seen the man for over five years, but his ghost still haunted me.

I couldn't hand the drugs back though. Not after Marcus has sought me out to work for him. And the money he was promising me was too good. So I swallowed the sick feeling and sold the drugs.

Turned out, I wasn't too bad at it.

And I knew how to interact with junkies. I spoke their language.

I could think about that first moment all night. That first time I met Marcus and let myself get sucked into this life. The promise of security and stability was everything I'd ever wanted.

That one moment changed everything. If I would have said no or walked away, who knows where I'd be now.

Surely not sitting in my Jeep, pining over Lana Romano.

John Vitale exits the club in the French Quarter, heading for my Jeep. Wordlessly, he slips into the passenger seat.

"Ignazio Vaccola," he says, his face stone-cold.

"John." I nod my head. "Sam told me to work with you."

John's head turns, looking me over as if he's assessing me. "Yeah, he told me he initiated you." He says it like a question rather than a statement. "And that you have Lana's best interests in mind."

My heart aches when he says her name. I rub my sweaty palms over the rough fabric of my jeans. "Something like that," I say.

"She's getting married tomorrow," he says casually, but his eyes are focused on me.

"I know."

He nods his head, leaning back into the passenger seat. "We had a plan," John says. "I don't know how much Sam told you though, it was a strictly need-to-know operation."

I assume I was not in the know, because I don't know what plan he's referring to. I assumed that Sam had some sort of plan, some sort of scheme to help his cousin, but I wasn't in on it.

"What was the plan?"

John shakes his head. "Doesn't matter now. It was contingent on Junior being alive." His eyes flash to mine. "And now he's not."

I rub a hand over my face.

I was right when I thought a war was brewing in New Orleans. But I had one thing wrong. I thought made men didn't kill each other. They're not supposed to anyway. I wanted this title so fucking bad, thought it would give me the protection I sought, but I was wrong.

There's no loyalty among thieves.

"Who killed him?" I ask. I know Sam was arrested, still in jail awaiting sentencing for the murder. But I can't believe he killed his own father. Their relationship seemed much better than the one I have with my father.

"I don't know," John says, a bit of venom lingers in his voice. He's pissed. Angry that this happened, and he doesn't even have a suspect.

I should have known better. The Costello children have spent the better part of the last two decades arguing over territories. It's a fucking civil war in that family.

And somehow I got caught in the crossfire.

"So what do you want from me?"

John looks at me with a sly smile. "You're from here, huh? Lived here your whole life?"

"Yeah..."

"Have you ever thought about leaving New Orleans?"

I don't know where he's going with this question, but I'm not sure I'm going to like it.

CHAPTER TWENTY-FOUR

Lana

MY REFLECTION LOOKS OFF. THE white dress clings to my body, the tulle skirt protruding from my waist. Madi buttons the back of the corset top with slow precision and my heart sinks further as she loops the hook over each white button.

Every moment feels like a step in the wrong direction.

But there's no turning back now.

The clock on the wall clicks away, each second passing by as my heart furtively pounds inside the cavity of my chest.

I feel empty, hollow inside, nothing to fill me up or bring me happiness. In order to make this marriage work I've had to rid myself of everything, empty out my body until there is nothing left but a shell of the person I used to be.

Because he can't break a person if there's nothing left to be broken.

That's the new plan. My poorly designed system. At least this way if I'm going to be unhappy it's on my own terms, and not because Davis won. Not because he controlled me.

Madi finishes with the buttons and stands tall, she looks me in the mirror over my shoulder. She doesn't say anything, probably doesn't even know where to start.

And honestly, I don't know what to say either.

She knows about my breakdown, what I tried to do. She laid in my bed with me after Naz was gone and my parents had given up on talking to me. Like always, Madi didn't ask questions, didn't give me a pretty speech or scold me. She just laid down beside me in silence, every so often squeezing my hand as if reminding me that I'm not alone.

I don't have the words to tell her what she's done for me. How her silent awareness has kept me moving forward.

I try not to dwell on hope, not to think about the good moments that I might still have. I don't want to have anything that Davis can take away from me. So

I don't confide in Madi, or let myself remember how good of a friend my cousin is.

I reach back, grabbing her hand and squeezing. Saying *I'm in here* without giving her too much.

I haven't met the new me yet, I don't know who Lana LaFontaine will be. I'm not sure what kind of clothing she'll wear or if she'll ever find a sliver of happiness, but I do know she'll always be haunted by Lana Romano.

No matter how well I box up the memories, or how good of a hiding job I do, I'll always have these moments of happiness lingering in the back of my head.

Images flashing through my mind of the moments that kept me alive.

Ice cream with Grandpa, parties with Lily, silence with Madi... and Naz. That one has too many facets. Grilled cheese and whiskey. Happiness and sorrow. Dive bars and the feeling of his leather interior against my skin while he fucks me. I'll remember the way his lips feel against mine, the heat that flushes through my body at the thought of him.

I'll always hold those moments close to my heart, even if I box them away and try to forget.

"They left to get mimosas," Madi tells me when she sees my eyes flicker around the room we're in. It's a large space in the back of the church, reserved for brides to get ready on their wedding days.

But it's just Madi and I in here. I didn't want a whole bridal party, and it was one of the few requests that was honored.

The door to the room swings open, I can see in the mirror as John enters without a knock. His eyes shift around the room before they land on me. He shuts the door behind him quickly.

"We don't have much time," he says, and I can sense the urgency that lingers in the words.

"What are you talking about?" I spin around, lifting the puffy dress as not to trip over the layers of tulle.

"Naz is outside in a black Ford Escape. You can walk out there, get in that car and never come back."

My heart stops. The steady drumming of it ceases and my jaw goes limp. "John," I breathe, "what are you talking about?"

It feels like the world has tilted off its axis. One second everything was spinning and leading toward the inevitable marriage, and then so quickly it stopped, the globe tilts, the spinning halts and I'm left here panting, unsure what to make of this new development.

It's too good to be true, so there must be some

catch, something I'm missing.

This isn't real.

I blink furiously, trying to make this dream go away before my emotions come back. Before I fill up with hope and give Davis something to prey on.

"You can be free, Lana. This is the only way I can help you. But if you get in that car, prepare to never be able to come back to New Orleans. Junior is dead. Sam is in prison. If I don't..." He trails off, leaving the words unsaid between us. But I know what he means. If he doesn't win this war, it's over. There will be no one left on my side. If he doesn't win, my parents will, and no one will be here to protect me. "You won't come back, understand?"

I can't say yes. I can't leave.

Family is everything.

Those words my grandfather said echo through my brain, bouncing off the walls of my skull. If I leave right now, if I take this out that John is giving me, am I abandoning my family?

"What about Madi?" I ask. Because if I leave, I'm leaving her behind too. What will she do without me, without an ally in her court? And what if Aunt Caterina forces her to marry Davis in my place? I can't do that to her.

"I'll take care of her. You need to decide now. Stay

or leave." John's words come out harsh, he's forcing me to make this decision without giving me a second to think about it. I need to weigh the options, assess the pros and cons. But his dark expression is focused on me and he's waiting for me to make the decision now.

I'm a prisoner here in this life. I'm adapting to their rules, trying to make the best of it but I know I will never find happiness here. I'll always be looking for an escape route. Staring at every rope and every knife wondering if that will be my way out.

But maybe, maybe I'm looking at my escape plan all wrong.

I've been copying Lily, looking at everything through the same lens as her. But her lens was broken, distorted. She took the wrong escape plan, I know that now. Because her way to freedom shattered me, crushed my soul and left me hollow.

I don't have to make that same mistake.

I can take a different path.

My heart races even though every fiber of my being wants to run out to that car with the man I love. But there's still something keeping my feet planted to the church floor.

"Take off the dress and run," Madi says. Her voice is strong and unwilting. She doesn't look unsure like me, instead she says the words in a demanding tone.

Madi steps to me quickly, grasping my hands in hers. "Go Lana. Run. And don't look back. You have a chance to have happiness. You shouldn't be standing here overthinking it, you should take it and drive off into the sunset. And if we never see each other again" — she shrugs her shoulders, but her eyes are glassy — "then that's okay. Because I'll always know that one of us made it out. Lily would be fucking thrilled that it's you."

I can't stop the tears that escape my eyes and roll down my cheeks, smearing the makeup that had been applied this morning.

"What will happen?" I ask John, even though my hands are still entwined with Madi's. My chest is aching from hearing Lily's name. Lily, who jumped over the edge of the balcony to prevent this day from happening to her. I should run if only for her memory, if only so no Romano sister has to walk down that aisle.

Fuck you, Davis, even money can't make a woman marry you.

"I'll take care of it," John answers.

"Go." Madi nudges her head in the direction of the door.

John looks at the gold watch on his wrist. "You need to do this now, Lana."

I spin for her to unzip the dress and she does. She tosses me my leggings and grabs a shirt from her bag. John turns as I slide the clothes up my body, pulling the sneakers onto my feet.

"Hold on," I say before John opens the door. I pull both of my cousins into my arms, squeezing them, knowing that this might be the last time I see them. "I hope we meet again," I whisper, and then John opens the door and I'm running.

Running through the entryway of the church, my sneakers pounding against the floor with a steady beat that matches the thrumming of my heart.

The church entryway seems empty, we were minutes from starting the wedding. I imagine the pews are filled with patrons that came here to celebrate this day. Congressmen and government officials coming here to wish Davis a happy marriage. I can't help but smile at the embarrassment that he'll feel when I don't walk down the aisle. What will his face look like when he sees my wedding dress in a heap in the dressing room?

It brings a smile to my cheeks and I can't stop it.

I can't prevent the rush of joy that fills my body, the tingling sensation as I let all of the emotions come rushing back in.

For a moment, I think Lily is running with me, a

huge smile etched across her cheeks and she shouts *we fucking made it out alive.*

My skin is on fire as I see the car, the black Escape staring at me like a beacon of hope.

Naz swings open the car door from inside, and I jump in, my body nearly flying into his from the momentum. I want to kiss him, to hold him, to feel my skin against his but I know we don't have time for that. Not yet.

Before I even close the door, his foot is on the pedal and we're moving.

I feel like we're flying, but it's just my adrenaline. Behind us I see the wedding planner standing on the street waving her hands. Trying to flag us down, trying to stop what's about to happen, but there's no turning back now. She'll call my parents first, I'm sure.

But I don't care.

I look at Naz's face for the first time. Scruff covers his jaw line and he's dressed in all black with a baseball cap.

"Stealing the bride?" I joke.

Laughter bubbles from his throat. "She never belonged to the groom," he says.

My heart melts a little. He's right though, I never belonged to Davis. My heart has always been my own, and I choose who gets my love.

"I love you, Ignazio," I tell him for the first time and the words feel like the first bit of truth I've spoken in years.

A red flush rises on his cheeks and he smiles at me as he navigates the car onto the freeway.

"I love you more, Lana."

CHAPTER TWENTY-FIVE

Lana

Ten Months Later

IT'S COLD IN NEW YORK City. The kind of chill I'd never experienced in New Orleans. At first, I didn't care, because the snow was mesmerizing. I could sit by the window and stare at the white flurry as it descended on the city.

But then I had to go outside, and the white slush soaked through my boots and the wind tunnel between the buildings made my ears bright red and numb. After that, I decided that I hated winter in New York.

Naz loves it on the other hand. Even now, as we tread through the slush, he has a child-like smile spread on his face as he stares up to the white sky.

Snowflakes stick to his dark lashes and his tongue darts from his mouth to catch the falling flakes. I can't help but to laugh at the sight, regardless of how cold my toes are.

We have an apartment, the thing about the size of my room back home, but it has tall windows and brick walls. In the morning we sit at the island counter, drinking our coffee and being thankful for the mundane days we spend together.

I hadn't realized how badly I craved boring. I wanted a routine, the same thing every day. Waking up to a snoring man with ruffled hair and morning breath. I wanted the feeling of binging Netflix together. The second we finish dinner and we land on the IKEA sofa.

It's mundane.

And simple.

And perfect.

On Fridays, we pour wine into the glasses I bought off the sale rack. Intertwining our arms and drinking it as if we're some sort of royalty, and then we laugh as we disconnect ourselves.

On Saturdays he sleeps in, and I get up first. Which is the opposite of during the week when he's up and out of the house before my eyes have even opened. He works as a mechanic at a shop down the street. He doesn't strip the parts from the cars, nor does he sell drugs to the customers.

We both have paychecks that go into an onshore bank account.

It's *normal.*

And while I know where every gun is stored in the house, each in a location easily accessible in case someone breaks in, the information slips into the back of my mind. I know there's a bag of cash in the closet and I have the account number of the offshore bank account memorized.

And while we're "free" from the New Orleans *famiglia*, New York keeps tabs on us as a favor to Sam.

There's a backup plan in case we ever need to use it. In case the family up here decides their loyalty would be better served to my parents.

But for now, I push those thoughts away, seal them up like the cash in the closet.

For now, I find happiness. Let the warmth of it radiate over me. I laugh at Naz as he rolls a snowball and fires in it my direction only for it to crumble midair.

We pawned my engagement ring.

It should feel wrong, and we didn't *need* the money, but there was something cathartic about it. The jeweler studied the ring with a magnifying glass, looking for any signs that it wasn't real. Neither of us flinched when he valued it at fifty grand. Davis wasn't cheap, and he had more money than he knew what to do with.

We took the cash and leased a small apartment for Naz's mother. Between the ring and the cash Naz had been saving we had more than enough to set ourselves and her up. She wasn't a fan of the idea of moving, but with both of her kids here, she eventually caved in.

I understood where she was coming from, she had lived in New Orleans her entire life, and now she was uprooting herself, moving to this new city. It was weird being so far from home, even weirder having no connections to home.

My runaway made the news. They even showed Davis' tear-streaked face. I wonder how hard it was for him to fake that.

No one's reached out to us though, no contact whatsoever.

I wasn't surprised to learn that Naz and John had plotted the escape together, leaving everyone else out of the loop. As long as we stayed here, no one would come to find us. But if we went back to NOLA, we'd be fair game.

For me, it would mean going back to my parents,

but it was a sure death sentence for Naz.

At first, the idea of never being able to go home ate away at me. I missed Madi and hated the thought of Lily's tomb being left unattended.

But I adjusted. The fresh start was more needed than I realized. I had become so used to living under my parent's thumbs, to having no life outside of the one they created.

New York was freeing. Naz and I decorated our small apartment for Christmas. Lugging a real tree up the steps and placing it in front of the window. We bought silly ornaments and anytime we saw one with an NYC landmark, we immediately purchased it and brought it home to add to our collection.

We strung Christmas lights throughout the apartment and in the evening we'd turn out the lights and shut the blinds, curling up on the couch under the golden glow of the lights.

I was mentally organizing all of the new memories, holding them close to my heart and replaying them in my head. It was as if I was catching up on all the things I'd missed over the years. All of the loving things you're supposed to do with your family, I needed to do them all as soon as possible. Needed to enjoy every second of freedom.

And family... Naz's was so much different than

mine. His mother was a sweet woman. She reminded me so much of my late grandmother. She spent her free time teaching me how to cook after I had mentioned my mother had never taught me.

Elly had some fancy job at a marketing firm where she wore cute blazers and high heels. Every time she stopped by, she looked happy. Stressed pretty often, but happy with her life.

And Anthony, my heart melts every time I see him and Naz together. His face shines every time the kid is over. They'll spend full Saturdays in front of the TV, working through endless levels of whatever game they're playing. Laughter echoing through the apartment.

I think this is what life is supposed to be like. Family, food, love.

In our first week here, Naz asked me what I wanted. I stared at him for a full minute, my mind completely blank. Unsure of what or who I was before. Before Lily's death, before my world was torn upside down. I have half a communication degree. I'm not even sure what I can do with that major. When I chose it, I didn't think it would ever matter. After Lily's death, nothing did.

But the colors have come back to my world, everything seems brighter and more vibrant. Suddenly I'm analyzing everything, wondering if it's something I want, if it's something I can do. I'm like a child, surrounded by endless opportunities.

Naz laughs as we pound our snow covered boots against the brick wall before we enter our building. "What's it today, *bella?*"

I roll my eyes. He finds my ever-changing hobbies amusing. Apparently while Naz was working for Sam he managed to make more money than we'd need for a while. Paired with the donation from John, and the cash we had on hand — we're set for a while. The money gave me freedom to take my time to decide what I wanted to do.

Which should be easier than it is. I'm overwhelmed with the ideas, and I want to do everything, soak up every possible experience. And when the thrill washes away, I move on. I'm becoming an adrenaline junkie for life.

"Writing," I tell him.

Since we've been in New York I've taken up reading as a hobby, devouring every word I can. After countless novels, I was ready to try something myself. Who knows, maybe I finally found my voice after everything.

He reaches forward, tapping the side of my blue light blocking glasses. "These are cute." He smiles.

"Very writer-ly, right?"

He laughs, leaning forward and pressing a kiss to my lips. "I love them."

Before he opens the apartment door he lifts me into his arms, carrying me through the threshold. Laughter escapes from my lips and before I know it he's tossing me onto the bed and climbing on top of me, kissing the few spots of exposed skin before he grabs for the zipper of my winter jacket.

These moments with him are my favorite, and I savor every second.

I wrap my arms around his neck, pulling him closer to me. "I love you," I whisper.

Hearing the words and saying the words never gets old. I could listen to his voice whisper those three words on repeat. I'm addicted to the love, the feeling that radiates between us.

He sheds me of my winter clothing and then removes his until we're naked in the bedroom of our apartment under the twinkle lights I'd strung up that week.

His fingers skim down, moving over my shoulder and down my torso finding my tit. Rolling the tight bud of my nipple between his fingers, he kisses me deeper.

I meet his dark eyes and they peer over my body,

admiring me in a way that still sends a shiver down my spine. I was afraid that at some point his gaze would stop affecting me in that way, but I'm still addicted to him. His admiration, his body, everything about him has me buzzing with energy.

Fingers skate over my arm, his touch searing me as it travels higher, stroking my cheek gently as he hovers above me. His thumb slips between my lips and I suck on the digit.

"Fucking beautiful." He breathes and dips his head lower, crashing his lips against mine. "Do you know that, Lana? Do you know how amazing you are?" He presses soft kisses along my jawline.

I don't tire of listening to his praise, his words send warmth through my body. His kisses trail lower, finding the hem of my leggings. He grips the stretchy material in his fingers, dragging it down my legs pulling them off. His hands rub over my legs as he settles between them.

His head dips down and my body tenses in anticipation. Every touch lights up my soul, sending sparks through me. His hot breath skates over my core and his tongue finds my slit. I moan as soon as he touches me. He finds my clit, licking the bundle of nerves and sucking it between his lips.

Everything with Naz is coated in warmth. His

soft encouragement and sweet words mixed with the dirty acts have me throbbing with need. I can still taste the saltiness of his skin on my tongue. I want more. I want his finger in my mouth, his lips on my skin, his cock inside me.

I want everything he has to give.

His fingers find my entrance and he pushes one in and then a second while continuously sucking on my clit. My fingers weave through his dark hair, gripping the locks between them while I cry out through my orgasm, falling over the edge.

He doesn't give me time to come down from the high before he has me flipped over, my ass popped up for him. He runs his hands over my flesh for a moment before he lifts one and brings it back down on the curve of my ass. I yelp out from the shock; he didn't hit hard enough for it to leave more than a little sting. With him, nothing feels wrong or dirty, I feel safe and secure.

He lines his cock with my entrance and thrusts inside me. Breathy moans escape from my lips as he pulls out and moves back in. In only a few thrusts my body is aching for him, wanting him to move faster, harder.

"Fuck," he moans. "You feel so fucking good, baby."

I warm at his words, the husky tone of his voice. My fingers reach back, grasping for him and his hand finds mine, our fingers interlocking.

"More," I pant.

I'm thrusting back against him, searching for the high that I've come to associate with Naz. Before him, I had never felt this energy, never knew what kind of light and warmth could exist in this world.

That first time he fucked me in his apartment, my body buzzing from the shots, he awoke something in me. I couldn't shove it back down after that, couldn't pretend that there wasn't something here, an electric current tugging us together.

We fit together so perfectly.

And he stood by me, even when I was promised to someone else. When being with me wasn't easy... or possible.

When I reach my orgasm, falling over the edge, I don't even hear the moans that leave my lips or the words I shout. I'm in a free fall, pure ecstasy.

Naz follows after me, pulling out and coating my skin with his cum.

We're sticky and panting when we finish. Naz goes to the bathroom, wetting a washcloth with warm water before coming back and cleaning me. He wraps me in a blanket, curling his body tightly against mine.

I'm surrounded by light, good things embracing me from all angles.

This is what I've wanted.

This is what I've dreamed of.

The buzz coming from my nightstand startles me, and I reach for my phone out of habit. The only people who call me now, on my new number, is Naz's family. But the number doesn't register. I don't think as I bring the receiver to my ear, murmuring a hello. I'm still coming down from my high, still soaking up the happiness I've found.

"Lana," John's voice echoes from the receiver. "Time to come back to New Orleans."

EPILOGUE

John

One Month after Lana's Wedding

MY EYES LINGER ON MARCUS as I bring the glass of whiskey to my lips. I can't be sure that he's not involved in...whatever this is.

I can see his eyes flicker to me. He's watching me, keeping tabs. We both distrust each other and with good reason, even though I like to think that my reasons are better, and *right*.

Right and wrong don't mean much to Marcus. Even as kids, he didn't give a fuck about doing the right thing. He's only ever cared about himself.

His grubby hands reach out to the stripper closest to him. One with blonde hair and fake tits. He pulls her down onto his lap and puffs on his Cuban cigar.

I guess the perk of owning a strip club is that you can do whatever you want with the women. What are they going to do? Tell the boss? Ha.

It takes effort for me to not roll my eyes or glare at him.

I can't. Can't let him get a whiff on where my loyalty lies. I made a big show of switching sides, of claiming to be loyal to him and not Sam. Even after he accepted me into his ranks, I could tell that he still distrusts me.

He's not wrong, because my loyalty will always belong to Sam.

The door to the private room opens and a petite girl with dark hair and bright eyes enters. She doesn't carry herself like the rest of the stripers here. She reeks of false bravado as she shuts the door with a soft click. A pair of tight leather shorts cling to her hips and her small tits are on display in a black lacy bralette. Cheetah print heels are strapped to her feet and around her ankles. She looks around the room with an assessing gaze, as if this is all new to her. And then, her eyes land on Marcus and something in her gaze shifts. I can't place the emotion, but it's not fear or loyalty, that much I can tell.

She takes a few steps, leading herself to the center of the room where one of the other girls is dancing.

I watch her as she sways for only a moment before taking another step, bringing herself closer to Marcus, who hasn't even noticed her.

What does she want from him?

I can't seem to take my eyes off her as she moves closer, waiting for the blonde to move.

"Can I get you something?" she asks, with a shy voice, matching the energy she's giving off. She's different from the other girls here, and not in a cliché way, it's clear to me that she's not a practiced stripper.

The girls in Marcus' club aren't normally newbies. The girls here are desperate, eager to please, *broken*. And this girl, she's not broken.

Marcus looks up at her with a confused face, the men around him having the same look. The women here don't talk to him unless spoken to, and yet, this little thing has the nerve to speak to him.

Part of me wants to lean back in my chair and watch the show.

"Excuse me?" His face tilts when he asks the question.

"This one new?" I cut in before she can answer, before she digs her hole any deeper. Her jaw snaps shut, and she looks at me.

"I dunno." Marcus shrugs. "You new, doll?"

She nods her head but doesn't open her mouth again.

"Can I test her out?" I ask Marcus, which brings some light to his gaze. Marcus has a favorite hobby of trying to loosen me up, trying to break through the composure that I pride myself on.

"Be my guest." He smiles widely, gesturing to the girl who now looks at me with an ounce of fear.

Finally, I think. The girl needs to smarten up.

I rise from my seat on the plush velvet bench and wrap my fingers around her arm, leading her back to a private room.

When I shut the door, she's looking at me with glassy eyes, fear lingering in her gaze.

"I'm not gonna fuck you," I mutter, loosening my tie. "What's your name?"

"Cat," she breathes.

Her name is most definitely not Cat, but I don't push her on it.

"What…what are…"

"Nothing." I answer the question before she's able to finish it.

She looks shocked for a moment. "Why?"

Because I need to gain my cousin's loyalty, make him think I've changed, that I'm more like him. I need to get him comfortable, so he spills all his secrets. And if he thinks I'm fucking her, then he'll believe me more.

I don't tell her any of that though.

Instead, I smile the best I can. "Because this is all a game, kitten, and I plan on winning."

Acknowledgments

Oh, man. Where to start?

You know how people always say it takes a village to raise a child? Writing a book is like that too, I think.

There's a lot of anxiety that comes with this process (at least for me) and I need a lot of people to work through that.

Jake- I will always thank you in the back of every book, even though you will never read them. That's okay, I still like you.

Alex- There aren't enough words in the English language to thank you. You've been my #1 supporter since day 1. Okay, maybe not day one since you hated having a sibling, but like at least for the last five years you've been great. Either way, thank you so much for being the best sister I could ask for, and thank you for only judging my writing subject a little bit.

Thalia- I've said it before, and I'll say it again: I couldn't do this without you! You're like my soul sister of writing. You cheer me on when I need it most and commiserate with me when none of my characters feel like talking. I'm so happy we found each other.

Anna- I can't thank you enough for being on this journey with me, you're the best hype woman I could ask for!

Laura, my kick ass beta, graphic designer, and amazing friend- I'm so happy I found you on this journey! You have been such a gem in my life and our chats keep me laughing. Love you!

Zainab, my editor and friend- Thank you for whipping this manuscript into shape and letting me know I'm a good writer even though I'm a terrible speller. You're amazing!

Julia, my AMAZING PA- Dude. Thank you thank you thank you from the bottom of my heart. I couldn't get these words out if I didn't have you taking care of everything in the background for me. Thank you for never sleeping and responding to messages within seconds. You are such a gem, and I'm so happy to have you!

Thank you to my amazing street team, Natalia's Famiglia, you guys are phenomenal! I appreciate you sharing my teasers and recommending my books, and I've enjoyed getting to know all of you!

And finally, to my readers, I literally couldn't do this without you. I mean, I could, but it would never leave my computer. I am so freaking thankful for every one of you who have picked up my books. From the bottom of my heart, thank you.

Also by Natalia

The Sinners of New Orleans

Alliance

Deception (Coming Fall 2021)

Obsession (Coming Soon)

Birthright (Coming Soon)

The DelGado Trilogy

Gio

Gemma

Gian

Stand Alones

Shattered

Velvet Lullabies

About Natalia

Natalia Lourose is an author of romantic suspense, dark, and mafia romance. She attributes her obsession with bad boys and criminals to watching far too much television and reading smut as a teenager. She calls Michigan her home and lives with her husband and three fur-babies. When not writing she can normally be found on tik-tok or some form of social media.

Printed in Great Britain
by Amazon

69237968R00189